Civil War II

E. Robert Gurr

ISBN: 9781096813569

First Edition

CONTENTS

PROLOGUE

JOHN HARTWICK

Why do you squint so hard John?

Hartwick looked over at his friend. Matt Davis had been with him from the start. He was one of the first people he had met when he moved to Indiana.

"I broke my glasses a few months ago. I had contacts, but they're gone as well. Can't find any glasses with my prescription. With all of the optometrists closed, and no deliveries, I guess it might be awhile." Hartwick answered.

"No!? Damn, I guess I never thought of that. Did you break them when you got shot in the face?" Davis asked.

"Yeah. It just cracked the left lens." Hartwick unconsciously raised his hand and rubbed the small scars on the left side of his face.

"I've heard there's a place outside of Dayton Ohio that's still running and can make glasses. But I haven't had the time to take a few days off and get over there."

"Nowhere around here is open?" Davis said.

"No. I guess the lenses I need all come from a few places in California and they can't get transportation. I tried online, but you know how that is now. I pay five or six hundred bucks and it might be here in three months."

"Well, you look like an idiot squinting like that." Davis smiled as he said it.

And then he walked away with the smile still on his face. Everyone was in a good mood.

It was nice. The last couple of months it had been calm. No fighting. Nobody dead or dying. Hartwick was standing just a few inches from a post next to a pharmacy just outside of Indianapolis.

The fighting here was long over. He leaned against the post to relax. Yet he was aware of every movement around him. That wouldn't end for a long time. He was always on the lookout for the enemy. His ears ever alert for the first bullet.

Too many had been wounded or killed by a lone sniper getting close enough to fire a few shots and then run.

He felt safe, but he was always aware. A civil war was a license to kill. Everyone could justify it. Neither side considered it murder. It was just war. So that brought the psychopaths out in the open.

He took a last draw on his cigarette and flipped it into the parking lot in front of him. "Cigarettes and beer." He thought to himself. Through all the hell of the last eighteen months, those two things were always available.

The sound of a car to his left caught his attention. He moved from the store and looked down the street. It was a black truck. Had to be one of their guys. It was moving too fast. Enemies tried to creep up on you.

Just to be sure he walked a few steps out towards the road and checked his holster to make sure he had the pistol. The Ruger Mini

14, a rifle, was slung over his right shoulder and had ammo in the magazine, but he wasn't sure how much.

"It's just the guys that went over to Ohio to meet with the Cincy group." He heard someone say.

That was good news. The men were back in less than a few hours. That meant they were organized and on the move from Ohio. He became aware of a rumbling behind him. Interstate 70 was less than a mile away. They were inside the 465 loop at one of the original rally points. No one knew why, but they always came back here before a big battle.

Hartwick himself had been back for just a few weeks. This is where it had started for him, and he hoped this is where it would end. His wife and kids were here. It was becoming peaceful.

He thought about the battles in St. Louis, Columbus, Atlanta and all those smaller cities in the Midwest. He had taken short trips to Pittsburgh, as far south as Atlanta and as far west as Des Moines.

At one point he had been away from home for three months. He thought of the people he had met. Quick friendships that were ended when a bullet took a life. In the bad days, twenty or thirty would die in a single blast. Thankfully that was all coming to an end. The local state militias that had been active for years had finally joined with them and everyone was organized.

The next battle would either end in victory or defeat. But either way, it would be over. If they lost, and Admiral Shock had double-crossed them, there was no telling what the future held.

He walked further out to the parking lot where a crowd of fifty or so had gathered to watch the buses. A few taunted insults at the prisoners of war inside the makeshift, chain-link fence prison.

They could see the overpass from where they stood. The rumbling was more than just one or two of the 18 wheelers that still passed every day or so. He walked out to the parking lot to get a better look.

It was a line of yellow school buses. Hundreds of them heading west. Others started to notice as well. The distinctive bright red X painted on the side of every bus. A loud cheer went up.

"Get them the hell out!" someone yelled.

Then even louder cheers. But Hartwick wasn't so sure this was a good idea. He knew there was nothing he could do. The buses were filled with the enemy, but at least they weren't being lined up and shot. He knew that had happened. And both sides, (was it really only two sides now?), had done it.

The buses were coming more often. Yesterday the yellow bus caravan had been twenty buses. That was a big one. Bus after bus loaded with those considered enemies and moved west. But today the line just kept going. There were hundreds of them. A few celebratory shots were fired into the air.

John Hartwick wondered if it was finally coming to an end. Or was this just the calm before the big storm? The battle was going to be huge. Even if he wasn't double-crossed, he knew many of his men moving across the country towards Richmond were going to die.

He made his way back to Matt Davis.

"How is Evans doing?" He asked.

"Good. Troy knows what's coming. He knows they are ready for us. But he still thinks we'll win."

"Well, of course they know we're coming. You can't move half a million men halfway across the country without someone figuring it out. Do we have any news on enemy numbers?" Hartwick asked.

"Not really. We are estimating the best case is a hundred thousand. Worst case could be as high as a million. If it's a million, our reserves will fill in and we'll still be evenly matched."

"What if they collapse that line on us?"

"We're sending a few diversions along the line to the north. But they're so far away I don't think it will matter. That's not the biggest issue anyway." Davis said.
"What is?"

"Just like we've talked about. The house to house stuff. If it comes down to that, Evans tells me we could lose half our army. Doesn't mean we still won't win. But that's a lot of dead Americans on both sides."

"I still think I should go." Hartwick said. "If I'm the top general, even if I'm just a political general, why shouldn't I be there?"

Davis shrugged his shoulders. "Evans and all the other guys with military experience say it's a bad idea. They want you here. We've got dozens of retired captains, majors, hell even generals helping us and making the plans. They know what they're doing. They'll call you if it's going well and we'll be on our way. I'd like to be there too. But, it's best we stay here for now."

"I'm going back home, Matt. I want to hug my kids and kiss my wife. I'll be back in an hour or so and we'll get ready for the call."

Davis stared at Hartwick and spoke very softly.

"John, I want you to know how much I appreciate all of this. I can't really find the words I want to say. I know what you did for me. I know what you've given up. I just want to thank you and tell you if something happens to one of us, I hope we meet again someday on the other side. I really do."

"I know Matt. I know. Me too."

Hartwick walked quietly to his car. He sometimes wondered how he had become the leader. But in his mind, kept buried, he knew. He had always been a leader. With every movement of his body and every word he spoke, he led. He had been born this way. He tried to tell himself that he had just lucked into it. That it had just been circumstance. But he knew that wasn't true.

He ran his fingers through his hair. In his early twenties he had noticed flecks of grey starting to appear. He hated it. But he kept it because it made him look older. Now in his mid-thirties it was grey all long his temples. He could pass for a good looking late forties. This got him respect. He was thin and almost six foot three inches tall.

Once he had worn cowboy boots with a two-inch heal. This made him over six foot five. He noticed that this gave him even more respect. He towered over most people with just that extra two inches. So from the first day in that parking lot he wore cowboy boots. He had assumed leadership. He wanted to lead that first group in Indianapolis. And now, he was leading roughly half the nation in a civil war.

CHAPTER 1

THE EARLY DARK DAYS

18 months ago

All twelve members of the FOMC of the Federal Reserve Bank were there. But in an unusual circumstance like this, they were meeting at the White House.

The President was in attendance as well as ten members of Congress. The Democrat candidate was also in attendance since the presidential election was just weeks away.

Conspicuously absent was the Vice-President. Hank Hoxworth was better known as Handsome Hank. A two-term congressman from Texas plucked by the President four years ago to be his running mate. He was one-quarter Mexican. His mother half Mexican and half Texan. His father was Henry Reese Hoxworth. The Texas oil magnate and once a candidate for President himself.

It was unclear who would win the election coming up. It was apparent who would win in four more years.

Hoxworth was tall, good looking, exceedingly wealthy and loved by the Republicans, Texans, most Mexicans, and secretly many Democrats.

He had graduated from MIT with a degree in engineering at the age of twenty. It was expected he would go to work for his father's company. But for ten years he traveled the world. He would be seen with Hollywood movie stars and leaders of nations. It was a common joke that there were no two pictures of him with the same woman.

Although the Democrats had tried to paint him as a dumb playboy, it hadn't worked. When Hoxworth was thirty his father died and he returned to Texas and took the reins of the business. The stock had fallen dramatically. So Hoxworth bought it at pennies on the dollar. Within five years the company had tripled in size. He was worth over ten billion dollars and controlled sixty percent of the stock.

When he finally settled down to marry he decided to run for Congress. To avoid any conflict, he turned control of his business over to the board and walked away. During the Vice Presidential debates it became evident that not only was Handsome Hank extremely likable, he was also brilliant. President Johnson's close victory was credited mostly to Hoxworth.

This was the reason the Democrats wanted him as far away from the meeting as possible. On this issue, they would not budge. He would be a distraction, and with the nation in such bad shape, it would be bad for everyone, they argued.

The economy was bad. As unemployment rose banks, were under more stress. Foreclosures were rising but the homes the banks owned were not selling. So new lending was also falling fast.

Protests had been growing more violent across the country. At first, it was fist fights. Over the last few weeks, sticks and knives had been used.

In Europe, things were worse. Paris, Berlin, and London saw daily riots. Fires were set and clashes between immigrants and citizens had grown deadly. As the economies in Europe and America stalled, China, South Korea, and Japan suffered as well.

The entire world was a boiling pot and governments were trying to keep the lid clamped down. The only thing the politicians could agree on was that things were getting worse. If the top blew off it was going to be bad. World war bad.

It was under this cloud that an election would happen in just two weeks. The Fed wanted to save the banks. The politicians engaged in elections wanted what was best for them. The tension in the room was overwhelming. The meeting was scheduled for 9:00 AM. As individuals trickled, in there was no small talk, no friendly banter. Just an eerie silence.

Everyone knew what the plan was. Print money. It wouldn't be called that. There was a small chance it wouldn't come to that. But few believed it. They were considering issuing over four trillion dollars in bonds. The interest rate would have to be raised meaning that the government wouldn't be able to sell them. Bonds would be given to banks and the money would be created from thin air.

The President and most Republicans wanted to cut spending. If they could pay unemployment benefits, social security, Medicaid and Medicare the nation would calm. For the first time, many

Republicans were calling for spending cuts in military spending. They also wanted cuts in every other department.

The Democrats wanted to raise taxes and borrow an additional trillion dollars. People needed help quickly, and they were promising that help. Their plan would put the deficit at over two trillion for the year.

The people throughout the country were just as tense as those in the meeting. Unemployment was growing by the day. It had happened so fast. All were sure the President would lose his re-election bid. But many were starting to worry the Democrat would be worse. The polls had Johnson losing badly. But as law and order began to break down, they were getting closer. Some showed the race within five points.

There were thirty people in the conference room. Two stood out. The President and a congressman named Victor Van Driessen were the only ones in the room with their heads up. Everyone else pretended to look at something significant on their phones, or were scribbling notes. The President was looking from person to person. His eyes rested on Van Driessen.

Van Driessen's face showed no emotion. He was leaning back comfortably in his chair. He noticed the President staring at him and nodded slightly.

The President began speaking.

"It's too close to the election to do something this radical. We have two weeks to go, can't we just wait?" He spoke to Jane Watson.

Watson was the chairwoman of the Fed. She was also frustrated, but for different reasons.

"Mr. President we just don't have the time. Lending has frozen up again and the troubles in Western Europe are aggravating the situation. This process has been done before. We are simply suggesting a repeat of 2008. It worked then and we have every reason to believe it will work again."

At the main table was the President and Doug Swindell, the Democrat who had won a fierce primary battle and was now ahead in the polls. The majority and minority leaders of the Senate were at the table as was the Speaker of the House and several other members.

The other members of Congress, chosen by committee sat in chairs around the outside of the table.

Victor Van Driessen was one of the most junior members of Congress and sat along the wall, outside the table. He was appointed by the governor of Virginia to finish the last six months of his deceased predecessor's term.

But in that short time, Van Driessen had made an impact on his fellow representatives. He was a Republican, but the Democrats grudgingly admitted the man knew economics and history. He could somehow put everything in context.

Outside of Washington D.C., few people had heard of him. But inside the Capital, everyone knew him. Every committee he was on and every speech he had been a part of had been doomsday hyperbole. Or at least that's what they thought initially. Now it was all coming true. From the widespread violence that had started across France and Germany, the credit crunch in Italy, Greece, Spain and once again France and Germany, to the current problems in the United States. Van Driessen had seen it all coming.

Other than the President, Watson, and Swindell no one had spoken. Until now.

"Just because it worked then doesn't mean it will work now. And did it really work? Isn't much of that money still floating around the banks propping them up?" Van Driessen said.

Everyone at the table turned to see who had spoken up.

The Vice President, Hank Hoxworth, had suggested Van Driessen. The two had met just a handful of times, but Hoxworth knew a smart man when he met him. Van Driessen would keep him informed and make sure that the politicians didn't screw it up.

The FED was supposed to fix this. It was a monetary problem, that's what they do. The Speaker of the House and his fellow Democrat Swindell, wanted to make sure the President and Republicans who controlled the Senate didn't screw it up. Swindell, was the governor of Vermont before running for President and had no idea who Van Driessen was, spoke.

"Uhh, Mister, I'm sorry I don't know your name, but this is what the Fed does. They have a good track record here, and I think we need them to, uhhhhhh, to sort of take the ball on this one."

Swindell smiled graciously, always in campaign mode, but Van Driessen wasn't moved. He had run his own business for thirty years. He knew a salesman when he saw one. And he knew a man who was full of shit when he heard him speak. He knew Swindell was full of shit.

"No, they have a terrible track record. And if the FED does this, we are going to find there are no buyers for the bonds. Same as last time. Only this time, they're going to have to print even more money and it won't help.

The people of this country are fed up, and they aren't buying it. They want jobs, stability, and security. This is going to get ugly." Van Driessen said.

FED Chairwoman, Jane Watson, tried to take control of the meeting. "Mr. Van Driessen, I'm sure you know we can always back the bonds. Inflation is still running at less than three percent. We'll do it the way we did the last time. We'll give the banks treasury bonds as loans. That way the inflation is tempered because the money won't circulate so quickly."

"It won't circulate at all." Van Driessen said. "You're just going to let them fix their balance sheets with worthless paper. But now, they have even less real assets than they did the last time. I'm telling you, you're going to cause a civil war if you do this."

Van Driessen was drowned out by a chorus of voices. "Let's not go there Vic, we're a long way from that."

"Easy congressman Van Driessen. No one is going to start a civil war over monetary policy."

Every voice but one was now speaking all over top of each other.

The President of The United States remained uncharacteristically silent.

Van Driessen let them calm down. He spread his hands apart in mock resignation and said.

"If you do as I suggest and cut spending, eliminate immigration, and add moderate tariffs, you'll lower the deficit and create some jobs. It may not fix the problem entirely, but it will help. And it certainly won't make it worse.

However, if you print money and it doesn't work, you'll cause hyperinflation or you'll expose our weakness to the bond speculators. If that cascades, all of these folks who are getting laid-off are going to have a tougher time finding a new job.

If you do this and bonds collapse, how are we going to pay for unemployment benefits? The last time we extended them. Will you be able to do that this time?

Look at the protests happening now. Two years ago it would have been college kids for the most part. Now you have middle-aged suburbanites coming into the cities to protest or counter-protest.

Do you know why? It's because these people believed in the system for their entire lives. They worked hard and paid their taxes. They have lovely homes and they had full bellies. Now, a few months after being laid off they aren't getting help. They don't get food stamps or unemployment checks as promised. Fat, content people aren't prone to violence. Lean and hungry men will fight. Those fat, lazy men you were trying to manipulate, are now lean and hungry"

The Democrat Speaker of the House protested.

"Congressman Van Driessen, I'm sure you realize that those few who aren't getting unemployment or food stamps is not because the nation is broke. We have the money. It's just the protests have slowed down the mail delivery and Government agencies in the city can't get to their places of work. We have the money. This will be fixed as soon as the election is over and the protestors go back home."

"Bullshit." Van Driessen said. "Tax revenues are way down and you know it. We're borrowing money illegally right now. Printing money illegally is the more proper term. A hungry man who believes he is having his life ripped away from him will fight. This will get worse if you don't fix it now."

Jane Watson was growing frustrated. "Congressman Van Driessen, your tariffs have been tried. During the Great Depression, the Smoot-Hawley tariff made things worse, not better."

Then the Senate Majority leader, a staunch Republican, added his thoughts, "She is right Mr. Van Driessen, this nation has always been for free trade. Tariffs cause prices to go up and other problems." He said it in a condescending tone but Van Driessen let it pass.

"You are both wrong. Completely wrong. Smoot-Hawley was probably too high. But even before that, we had about a thirty-five percent tariff. And all through the nineteenth century, we had tariffs.

When Smoot-Hawley was repealed in 1937, the nation sank into another depression within the Great Depression. We are sending more money out of the country than the growth of GDP. Do you not understand that this cannot go on forever?

You can't bring millions of immigrants into the country to compete for jobs and lower wages, then send millions of jobs overseas and have them done by people making one dollar per hour, and at the same time, have no tariff on those products coming in. For the love of God, pick one! But get at least two of the three feet off of the necks of the middle-class.

There was no response to his question. There was a motion to have an unofficial vote. Just minutes later the FED voted along with the politicians to bail out the banks and try to stimulate the economy. They all agreed to speak as one voice praising the decision. All but Van Driessen.

When asked if he would at least keep quiet he just shook his head softly and walked out. He stopped at the door and turned to look at everyone in the meeting. His eyes moved slowly from person to person.

"This will not work. You seem to believe that violence is something that only happens in the inner cities. You think that the nice white people in the suburbs and rural areas are more civilized. You are wrong.

The inner cities are violent because they lack hope, they feel beaten down and irrelevant. You will soon find that all human beings can be reduced to violence. The most dangerous animal on the planet is a man filled with righteous indignation and an empty stomach.

You are renting out your minds to yesterday's thinkers. Not one of you came up with an alternative idea. Not one of you even suggested another path may be better. I hope that your plan works. I want it to work. Civil unrest, violence, and civil war are horrible. No one wins.

You believe it cannot happen here. You are wrong. Western Europe is burning. We've had protests and riots for months here in The United States. This will get worse."

And with that, he left.

There were a few nods of disbelief at this crazy old man who had somehow ended up in Congress. Most believed he was wrong but they were afraid to speak up. All hoped that he would not win the election for a full two-year term on his own. They knew that if he did, he would not keep quiet.

As the group started to pack their papers and began to shuffle out of the meeting they noticed the president had not moved. The entire group paused to look at him and see if he had something to say. His head was bowed slightly and he was rubbing his hands together in deep contemplation. He too had approved of the plan to bail out the banks and stimulate the economy.

The Federal Reserve Chairwoman felt compelled to speak because everyone else was just staring awkwardly. "Is there something else Mr. President?"

Bill Johnson, the first time politician and president of The United States raised his head slowly and looked directly into her eyes.

"Are you sure this is going to work?"

Jane Watson offered a soft and slightly condescending smile. She had fallen into the trap of most high-level Washington insiders over the last few years. She thought she was smarter than the politicians.

"Mr. President, nothing is certain of course. But this is the best tool we have to keep the economy afloat until conditions improve. This is tried and tested and will, despite some objections from newer members, not make things worse, and will help. Will it fix it completely? Again, nothing can be 100% certain. But it will help tremendously. Of that, we have no doubt."

The president smiled and nodded. 'She has said nothing, and she has no idea.' He thought to himself.

CHAPTER 2:

NOVEMBER

The news anchors, the pundits, and the politicians were exhausted.

It was Two O'clock in the morning, and no one could determine who had won the presidential election. The talk was mostly about the protests and riots that had broken out in nearly every city in the country.

President Johnson was ahead in Wisconsin by less than 500 votes. Those 500 votes, if they held, would give him an Electoral College victory and he would remain President of The United States.

He had lost the popular vote in spectacular fashion. More than five million people had voted for Swindell than Johnson. But the entirety of the margin was from California. Something was wrong in California. Nationwide it had been a high turnout election. Over sixty-six percent had voted. But in California, the number was nearly eighty percent.

Victor Van Driessen sat alone in his house. His wife had passed years ago, His two children raised and long moved away. By 8:00 PM it was clear he had won his first full term in Congress.

There had been national media focused on the race. The sixty-seven-year-old Republican should have lost to his challenger handily. It was a split district that had been leaning left. Van Driessen had been painted in the media as a hard right lunatic. He had been called a racist, bigot and an old fool.

He had won with just over sixty percent of the vote. Something he had said had resonated with the voters. People were frightened.

He watched television flipping from Fox News to CNN as the talking heads droned on. It was clear no one knew what the outcome would be. He turned off the television just as the phone rang.

"Mr. Van Driessen, this is, well this is President Johnson. I wanted to call and congratulate you on your win. I hope I didn't wake you."

Van Driessen was instantly wide awake. This is a call he wasn't expecting. He had never spoken privately to the President before.

"Oh, well thank you, Mr. President. And it looks as if congratulations are in order for you as well."

"Maybe, but that's part of the reason I called you Vic. May I call you Vic?" He asked.

"Sure Mr. President."

"And why don't you call me Bill. I want this to be off the record and informal. When we were in that meeting a few weeks ago, you said you thought that the Fed's action would cause a civil war. How serious were you with that comment?"

Van Driessen paused for a long moment. He knew this phone call was important, he just didn't know where it was going.

"It's not just the Fed's action Mr. President. It's that this isn't going to work. We have high immigration and have had that for years. We have stagnant, or at best, slowly growing wages. And we've had that for years. We also have a massive imbalance in imports and exports. We've tried to trick the middle class into thinking they still have money. But they don't. We've let them, hell we've encouraged them, to keep borrowing to keep the mirage going.

So when the Fed prints the money this time, the average Joe may believe it worked. And may go about his business. But the business owner and the investor know better. They may not understand it correctly, but they know the FED is printing money. And they know that means their money won't be worth as much. So they are going to start laying people off and stop investing. They are going to want to hold cash and hard assets. And God only knows what the bond buyers are going to do.

Sir, I think it's a recipe for disaster. And yes, if it doesn't work, and I don't think it will, I believe there is going to be hell to pay. A civil war? It may not come to that, but nothing right now suggests that it won't."

"And now we have these election problems." The president added.

Van Driessen paused again. He had the same thought just minutes ago and tried to put it out of his mind. He needed to relax. This was an important conversation.

It was clear President Johnson was starting to understand how divided the nation really was. He wanted the President to trust him. Maybe this could be stopped. Perhaps civil war or widespread violence could be avoided.

"Mr. President, I was just thinking the same thing."

"So, if a few votes more came in for Swindell, and I conceded, that would stop a recount, and maybe it could bring the country back together. I keep looking at the news from Europe. Those protests get more violent by the day. I think that is what is driving some of the division here. If I stepped away wouldn't it help?" The president offered.

"No. please don't do that. I know some of the people around you are probably suggesting that, but it's a bad idea."

"No one has suggested it." The president said. "But I can feel it. And I think it may be the best course of action. Swindell did win the popular vote. Not by the margin they are saying. We know there was widespread fraud in California and North Carolina.

We can't challenge North Carolina because we have our own problems there. But the data guys are telling me we actually won. Swindell finished about four-thousand votes ahead, but I am being told we should have won by ten thousand.

There isn't much we can do about it. California, I lost. But, they are telling me that millions of votes are just not possible. So I lost the popular vote and the electoral vote is hanging by a thread. I don't want to see this country tear itself apart Vic."

"You lost California, and Connecticut, Vermont, New York, and Massachusetts as well. But let me ask you, how much time did you spend campaigning in those states? How much money did you spend advertising? You campaigned to win the Electoral College. And you did. Would it have been better had you sunk resources in those states, won the popular vote and lost anyway? Do you think the left would be screaming to let you be president?"

The president was silent for a long time. "I just don't want my presidency to be the cause of violence. This is a great nation. The greatest that has ever existed. I know that in my mind and my heart. I just want to do the right thing."

"The right thing is to follow the law, Mr. President. The right thing is to fight. If you quit, you'll solve nothing. Your supporters on the right already don't trust the government. They trust you. They will never accept it if you quit.

If you fight and win, and if the economy doesn't slow too much, we will probably be able to avoid violence. Hell, we may be fine no matter what happens. We aren't going to go back to the Stone Age even if the economy falls drastically. People may be just comfortable enough to stop short of violence. At least for a while. But if you concede, and it's perceived as a surrender, things will get worse. Much worse. Of that I am sure."

"There's something else Vic." The president added.

"At about four this afternoon I got a message from the Fed. The bonds aren't selling. They think we're going to have to raise the rate by a full point. That means this is going to cost us a lot more than we planned for. We're also hearing that it looks like unemployment by the end of the month is going to pass twelve percent. That's a full three points up from just one month ago."

Van Driessen thought the unemployment number was a foregone conclusion. The bond issue shocked him. It should have taken a few months for that to happen. This was a bad omen coming so quickly on the bailouts.

"More reason to fight Mr. President. If you concede I think it will make things worse."

The two men talked for more than an hour. They spoke about the widespread violence in France and Germany. They discussed the slowing economy and trouble in China.

It seemed as if the entire world was simmering and about to blow up. The economy in The United States was clearly heading down, but it was much better than just about anywhere else in the world.

When the conversation ended, Van Driessen was happy that the President had decided not to concede. He would fight.

But he was more concerned about a civil war. The President had told him other things that were about to get worse. The unemployment rate was going to continue to rise. The ability of the government to borrow more money, which would be necessary for unemployment benefits, food stamps, Medicaid and Social Security wasn't going to be easy. With Europe's problems and now apparently issues in South America, the economy was going to shrink even faster.

The protests in Europe were growing. The European Union was being ripped apart at the seams. Germany was softening its unemployment problems by bringing hundreds of thousands of young men into its army. France was starting along the same course. Those two nations were working together to put pressure on Eastern Europe to take in some of the millions of immigrants.

What if war breaks out in Europe and civil unrest, or civil war happens in The United States? Van Driessen didn't want to think about it.

But the biggest news to break was that some of the Republicans were suggesting extensive deportation. The thought process was logical. If the president was right, and the economy was going to get worse, it meant they weren't going to be able to provide for the citizens, much less thirty million immigrants. Democrats had gotten wind of the plan just yesterday. Too late to make it an election issue. And they were vowing to stop it.

Van Driessen was sure this was going to be all over the news and the left would use it to try and push President Johnson to concede. Things were going to get ugly. Would millions of immigrants, both legal and illegal, join the protests? If they thought they were going to be deported, they would fight.

If the left thought the election had been stolen from them, they would fight.

Then there were the millions that had lost their jobs or might over the next few months. What would they do? Who would they blame?

The nation was a powder keg. But those who could stop it from exploding were afraid to do so or didn't know what to do. The men like Van Driessen and Vice President Hoxworth who might have had a workable plan were powerless.

Van Driessen walked back to his bedroom and laid down in bed. He was staring at the ceiling. The President was a bombastic man. He would fly off the cuff at times with a terrible temper. He didn't trust anyone but his own inner circle. He was thought to have an incredible ego, which was saying something in Washington D.C., they all had huge egos. And yet he had considered conceding. He would walk away if he thought it would help the nation.

Van Driessen wondered if the President was right. Had he given the President bad advice? It was nearly impossible to sleep. He could see no path in his mind to avoid what was coming. If the president conceded and things fell apart, the right would want blood.

If the President won, even if the economy turned around, the left would feel like the election had been stolen from them. So they might fight. But if they won and the economy collapsed, everyone might want to fight.

The news of the Republican plan for deporting immigrants was also a risk. It would save money. There was no doubt it would help. But the Republicans would take a beating from the media and the Democrats. Was it right to send millions of people back to countries where things were probably even worse?

Van Driessen sat up and put his head in his hands. He had only been in politics for a few months. In that time he realized that ninety percent of what politicians fought about was silly and easy to resolve. It was made complicated only by politicians.

This was different. There was no easy answer. For the first time, Van Driessen could not see a path to a peaceful outcome. No matter what happened, roughly half the nation was going to be outraged.

There was only one question left. Of those that were going to be outraged, how many would fight?

Van Driessen was sure of one thing. The fuse had been lit. There was no way to avoid the fight that was coming. His mission in life would be to stop it from turning in to a civil war. Nothing else mattered.

CHAPTER 3

COLBY OHLBINGER

C olby Ohlbinger was wide awake. The sun was coming up, and he knew he was at the center of the storm.

He had been glued to the television and his phone since He'd left the polls at 9:30. They had faked a few ballots. Maybe a few hundred at most. But it wasn't enough. The Republicans had cheated, he knew it. He and his cohorts had cheated for the Democrats and they told each other they were justified in doing so.

There would be a recount. But that was out of his control. The mission now was to lead. Too many of his friends and associates wanted to wait for the recount, and then start the protests if they lost. Ohlbinger knew they had to begin tonight. He had all day to prepare. Johnson hadn't conceded and his Democrat opponent Swindell hadn't conceded. The battle for the future would take place here in Madison Wisconsin.

He had already called the High school where he worked as an English teacher and told them he wouldn't be in for work. Too much to do. They had understood completely.

He spent the day in furious, focused activity. By Five O'clock they had to be in place. There would be a crowd of people leaving work for home. The national news would still be all about the election, but it would be before prime time. He was organizing a protest, but he badly needed this to become a riot. If it flamed out, he would spend a few nights in jail and his parents would need to pay some fines.

At twenty-nine years old, and on a teacher's salary, he didn't have much money. But his mother and father were also intellectuals. Academics who knew the importance of his work. They were at their vacation home in Florida. But he could easily have them transfer money before they got home to Madison.

The crowd he had assembled was bigger than he had hoped. Over ten thousand had already shown. He knew more were on the way. Many if not most from out of town, but they were flooding in by the minute.

When the news broke that not only was the election in doubt but that there was a plan by the Republicans to throw thirty million people out of the country, more people had decided to protest.

He grabbed the megaphone and walked to the podium just erected. They had no permits. This was the start of a revolution. This was just. He would lead.

"My friends."

Colby started softly. He wanted the crowd to listen. He wanted them focused on his every word. These protests were always tough. Too many people with too many different issues. Everyone chanting slogans related to their own cause.

But the crowd fell instantly silent. He paused for nearly a minute.

In that short minute, he thought about his life. His father, a quiet man who left the discipline of Colby to his wife. When he spoke, he told Colby to try to do the right thing.

His mother. A radical and motivated liberal who wanted her only child to be a political leader.

The fight. When he was eleven years old, Colby had beat up a boy who was only nine. It was one of the few times his father had ever been disappointed in him.

"You should not pick on someone younger and weaker than you."

That was all his father had said to him. He had beaten up little Timmy Douglas. A kid that lived next door. Timmy's father owned a business and was rarely home. Timmy, although two years younger, was a better athlete than Colby. He did better in school. Timmy had been moved up a grade, and Colby had been held back. So they were in the same grade, and that year, the same class.

Timmy had done better on a test, and in a fit of jealous rage, Colby had fought him at recess. He had won, but it had been closer than he thought.

Colby's mother had at first feigned anger. But when they were alone, she had winked at Colby and game him a punishment of no desert. They never ate desert anyway.

Two years later, when Colby was thirteen and Timmy was eleven, they fought again. This time Colby was beaten badly.

Colby's mother had been outraged. She threatened Colby's parents with a lawsuit.

Colby's father had said nothing. From that point in his life, Colby was two people. The son his mother wanted him to be. Often ruthless in his pursuits. And the son his father wanted him to be. Helpful to others, kind and honest. Today, he knew he was his mother's son. He shook the thoughts from his head and continued.

"They are trying to steal our country."

And then the crowd erupted. He had to manage this. He let them scream for just a few seconds and raised his hand to silence them. The crowd instantly hushed, surprising Colby again.

He needed to make a quick change. His mind went back to the great speeches he had read. He had to control this. He had to let it build slowly over time. Let the rage build.

He knew if he uttered President Johnson's name, or the Republicans, he would lose them. They would start shouting and screaming, and then they would dissipate into their own little groups of anger.

The Pro-Choice groups would peel off, the environmentalists would form another small group and on and on.

He had to keep them together. He had to get them interested and get them to shut up. Instead of throwing red meat, he decided to change course. He didn't want anger from them. Not yet.

"We are on the cusp of a great victory."
Again he paused and scanned the faces in the crowd. There was confusion. That's what he wanted.

"For so long, we have worked so hard. For so long we have been civil and patient. Despite the gerrymandering, we have won. Despite the cheating, we have won. Small victories at first, but then bigger and bigger.

When we have lost the presidential elections, it has all too often been a loss because of some arcane electoral college system rooted in old traditions, from old men, from another age."
He had planned on hitting the white supremacy points here but decided to soften it.

"We have had setbacks. But we have persevered. We are standing at the door of a just and righteous nation. We have prevailed. And now, as we are on the cusp of the final victory, I can see that some of you are willing to let it all slip away. Many of you are here for your own interests and for your own groups.

My friends, we must come together. We are one group. We are one united people, and we only want one thing."

He let the air still. He saw the faces focused intently on him. They wanted to know what the thing is they all wanted. A smile slowly came across his face. This was the moment. If he got it right here, he had them. He had his army.

"We simply want what rightfully belongs to us. That is all. For too long we have been the ones to struggle with injustice among our minorities. We are the ones who have struggled to make ends meet while the millionaires throw us their spare change.

Let me ask you friends. If we had the money that was owed to us would we have the problems of crime? If we had the money that the billionaires are hoarding, would we have so much trouble paying our bills? If we had the money they took from us, would our voices be silenced?"

Ohlbinger's voice was still soft. He kept it purposefully low and quiet. He wanted them to strain to hear. To make sure they could hear his every word. He wanted them calm and compliant in the moments before the explosion.

He could feel the energy building. The crowd was visibly moved. They were shuffling and nodding their heads.

"And now!"

He screamed at the top of his lungs. The crowd to a person was startled and as one stepped back.

"And now that we have our victory they want to steal it from us?! The moment our payment is due and ready to be delivered they want to snatch it from us?

Again?!"

The crowd was getting angrier by the word. Ohlbinger paused and bowed his head. After a few seconds, he simply started shaking his head back and forth, back and forth. He dropped his voice again.

"No, my friends. No, my fellow patriots. No, my fellow warriors. Not this time. Not this time."

He raised his head slowly. "We have had enough. We have had our birthright stolen from us for the last time. We will not be abused again. This is wrong. It is time for us to fight. It is time."

The murmur of the crowd was growing. Colby had only minutes before he lost them. It was time to seal the deal.

"Do not quit. Do not give up this time."

They quieted slightly. So he raised his voice again.

"Do not let the person standing next to you give up. Be the strength they need. They want you to do this! They want you to help them fight. Do not go to work this week. There is food all around us. Take it! It belongs to you anyway.

We must fight. We must stop this fraudulent recount from happening. We know who won. We know who cheated. Don't let them put on their little show! Don't lie down again. Don't surrender again.

You have been beaten and beaten and abused by President Johnson and his dirty Republican troops. Rise up and fight back! It is your country, it is your money and it is your life that they are stealing!

Do not let the cowards and the plants alter your course. Oh yes, there are plants among you. There are FBI agents and Republican operatives. You will know them because they will try to get you to quit. They will urge you to be peaceful. The will suggest that there is time. They think you are cowards. They think with a few words and a pocket full of change you will go quiet again. When you see those cowards, know that they are infiltrators. Drive them out!"

The crowd was in a frenzy. It had not gone as he had planned, but it had worked. Now the rest of the act had to be completed. He knew every step from here perfectly.

He looked at the crowd in disgust. He wanted them shamed. He wanted them to fight. If they did not, they were cowards.

He threw down the megaphone violently and stormed off the platform. He had told his close group that when he did this, they were to follow him and get others to follow.

The entire group marched to the center of the city.

"This city is closed! This nation is ours!"

He started a chant, and the rest followed. He knew he would lose some. They were unimportant. By the weekend he would see the size of his army. He reached into his pocket and pulled out the perfect rock. He had spent so much time and had so much attention to detail even the rocks he picked had been meticulously selected.

There was one in each pocket. Only two. The first throw had to be perfect. He walked close to the largest window he could find. In a strange twist, it was the offices of the headquarters of the Democratic Party. He did not know this, but it would become the luckiest thing he had done. He let the rock fly through the window. The crowd picked up the cue, and the rioting began in earnest.

That night, the entire national media led with the Wisconsin riots. The rock going through the window of the Democratic Party, they said, had been a warning not to the Democrats, but to all politicians. They would not be subdued. They talked about the young, energetic and passionate leader Colby Ohlbinger.

The recount in Wisconsin was temporarily halted. Over the next days and weeks, people from all over the country came to join Colby Ohlbinger. They came to say that enough was enough. They would not be cheated again.

Small tent cities cropped up in parks and even along the broad sidewalks. CNN, MSNBC, Fox News, even the major networks had come to Madison. They all wanted to interview Ohlbinger. There were over two-hundred thousand protesters crowded in to the city.

But it was getting cold. And he was getting bored. He also knew that he could not lead a revolution from Madison. He had to get to Portland Oregon. The protests there had been more violent and the police were starting to crack down.

He was sure there were enough supporters to keep Madison disrupted. They just needed to maintain. But if he was to truly lead he had to make it to the west coast.

On December 1st he left Madison quietly. He selected a group to lead in his absence and told them he would be back soon. He took five people with him. Two young girls, a Hispanic man, an Asian kid he hardly knew and one other white man. His sometimes confidant Steve Oxley.

He didn't trust Oxley completely, but he knew him better than just about anyone else. His diverse group had just the right mix. One of the young girls was a radical lesbian.

Colby knew she wasn't so much committed to the cause as committed to destruction. She was utterly unfocused but violent to a fault. The others were sycophants. Other than possibly Oxley, who seemed a bit too contentious.

They landed first in Seattle. This was by design. It was merely to build his credibility. The only person he had notified, outside his small group, was a reporter for CNN. She would be waiting for him at the airport and accompany him to the center of the protests in the city. He gave one speech, virtually the same speech he had given in Madison. He then mingled with the crowd and had dinner with some of the leaders.

Colby didn't listen to anything they said. He dominated the conversation, told them to fight at all costs, and be on the lookout for the cowards and the infiltrators. He knew what he was doing was right. He wanted to help these people. But he knew he had to push them. If he didn't the left would lose again. He was tired of losing.

He left the restaurant without paying his share of the bill or that of his team. But he left them with the impression that he was in charge, and revolutions needed leaders.

And then they left by car for Portland. He had no money for plane tickets. He knew the rest would take care of itself.

By the time he made it to Portland, he was becoming more famous. CNN had led with his surprising appearance in Seattle. The crowd had been energized. He was greeted as a savior by the committed. The protests had been dwindling.

Those who study history understand the importance of luck. Luck can win a battle. Luck can elevate a mediocre person to leadership in the blink of an eye. Colby Ohlbinger was about to get very lucky.

This was where he would make his bid for national leadership. CNN had scooped everyone with his surprise visit to Seattle.

So earlier in the day, as he was driving into Portland, he called every media contact he had made. He would be giving a significant speech the following day at 6:00 PM.

This would provide the media with time to talk about what was coming. It would also allow time for fellow fighters across California, Oregon, Washington, and anywhere else they may be, to assemble.

The first bit of luck came from the Supreme Court, and it was good news. Good for Colby at least. The protests in Madison would make it impossible for any kind of an accurate recount. Thus the election night results would hold, and Johnson would win his second term as president.

The bad luck, which would also benefit Colby, was that the people of Wisconsin had had enough. The police were moving in from all over to clear out the protesters. It was becoming clear that if he wasn't there to lead, the protests would all apart.

A growing show of force by the police from many different cities was converging on Portland to restore order there as well. But with Colby's arrival, they had been ordered by the mayor to stand down for a few days.

The crowd in Portland was primed. This time he didn't need a cheap megaphone. A microphone and speakers had been set up.

The crowd stretched as far as he could see. Several local radio stations were also carrying his speech live. Once again he started his speech softly. In fact, he started without saying a single word. He just bowed his head shook it back and forth, over and over. Finally, he looked up and let his eyes scan the crowd.

"I told you this was going to happen." He said softly.

He kept his eyes on the crowd. Scanning faces and accusing them all. Accusing them of being weak. Accusing them of being cowards. No words were spoken, but all knew the message he was conveying.

"I told you this was going to happen!" He screamed at the top of his lungs.

Mayor Sheila Everson was sitting with Colby's group of five, and another five local leaders at the podium. She was a lifelong Democrat and self-avowed social justice warrior. Everson had invited one council member to the podium as well, and Colby had thought it a great idea to show solidarity. She felt her presence would soften Ohlbinger's rhetoric. She had miscalculated.

"Have we finally had enough?" He continued. Not yelling anymore, but his voice filled with passion. He was on the verge of tears.

"Have we finally been lied to enough? Have we finally had enough stolen from us? Have we finally come to the point where we will no longer lie down?"

The rock that he had thrown through the window of the Madison Wisconsin Democrat headquarters window came back to his mind. When he found out the window he had broken was Democrat party headquarters he had thought it a huge mistake.

When he heard what the media was saying about it, he was confused. Why would he challenge the Democrats? They may not be much in his eyes, but it was the only team he could play for, wasn't it?

And then it hit him. That awful stroke of good luck. He could take that party right now. He could run it from anywhere in the country. Any decision they made would have to go through him. They would be forced to fight for what was right.

He turned and stared at the mayor. The sixty-year-old, former human resources executive for a large tech company, nodded and smiled. She was a tiny woman with perfectly styled gray hair. She preferred leaving her reading glasses on at all times and peaking over the top of them. Clapping her hands, she gave Colby a thumbs up. Mayor Sheila Everson was nervous. She had told her security detail not to come to the podium, but to stay close.

Colby pulled the microphone from its stand and walked over to her. His mind was racing. He knew he had to get this right.

He put a soft smile on his face as he approached her. They had met briefly just before the speech. He had been polite and respectful to her.

His smile put her momentarily at ease, and she stood slowly. And the smile on Colby's face turned to a sneer.

"Are you going to fucking help us this time?" He screamed at her.

Frightened, she stumbled back and fell into her chair. The fall startled Colby as well, but he quickly recovered. The crowd roared their approval.

"Or are you another plant?" He screamed again. He turned and stepped back to the microphone.

"We cannot abide by any more of these politicians who tell us they will fight for us, and then go back to their dinners with Republicans, billionaires and other thieves."

He paid no attention to the security detail behind him removing the mayor and the other members of city council. When he caught them out of the corner of his eye, he stopped and watched.

"Good! Take them away!"

He said it as if he was directing the security team.

"We need no more politicians who are unwilling to stand with us. Leaders who are too cowardly to fight with us must be weeded out. We need no more of the bought and paid for politicians. Let the billionaire's puppets hide as they always do.

I came to Portland to fight with you.

We came!"

He turned back again to acknowledge the other supporters remaining on the podium behind him.

"We have no money. We spent our last few dollars on a cheap hotel room that we will share. We have no money even for dinner tonight. But we don't care! We are here to fight. And when the fight is over, and we have won, all of us will have full bellies, nice homes, and free health care! All of us will win!

This time we aren't going to let you infiltrate our ranks! This time and in this place, the line will hold! Madison was the beginning of the battle, Portland is the center!"

He ranted for thirty minutes. When the crowd was sufficiently angered he led them to the center of the city, and to the mayhem.

Katana Coolidge, the warrior lesbian, had been briefed on what to do. He needed her first and foremost to start by burning his rental car. Then he wouldn't get stuck with the bill.

She did as directed and the long weekend of rioting began in Portland.

After just an hour Colby left for his motel. His car was burned and unusable, so he had to walk. The other four, along with two of the local leaders joined him back at his room.

He sat down on the bed and feigned exhaustion. "God I'm hungry and tired." He said. This is where he turned on the charm. Within minutes one of the local leaders had ordered pizza and made a few other phone calls.

Colby knew that people couldn't always be riled up and angry. When there were smaller groups, things had to be relaxed. Then they would relate that peace and calm with being with him.

He needed time alone to plan for tomorrow, but he would not get the chance.

The man who had bought the pizza, he looked to be late in his thirties or early forties, stood and made a brief speech about the day's events. He asked if he could have a moment alone with Ohlbinger.

Colby smiled. "Sure, sure, but I always like at least one of our other leaders to stay. I want all of us to be able to trust each other. Sox, why don't you hang back?" He suggested.

Sox was Steve Oxley's nickname. Colby didn't really care who knew what he was up to. But he was a little nervous that he had crossed a line and the Portland leader, he thought his name was Don, but he really didn't remember, was going to chastise him. Don was a bit bigger than Colby and the last thing he needed was a physical fight with one of the locals.

Oxley nodded and sat back down in one of the little chairs against the window.

As soon as everyone but the three had left, Don told him why he wanted to talk to him.

"Look Colby, you're doing great stuff here. Really great stuff. The resistance has always needed a strong leader. Someone had to be the figurehead to carry our message.

But you're not going to be successful if you don't have any money. I've made a few calls to some of the Hollywood folks, and wealthier supporters and they really like what you're doing.

I've asked them to meet us here and they should arrive any minute. I think you'll like what they have to say, and they can give you a few bucks to get you into a nicer hotel and maybe some money for a little food and other things you may need."

"Well, I don't know what to say." Colby said. "We did coast into town on fumes and spent our last few dollars on this hotel. I just figured I could find a part-time job to keep me going as long as I could to help here."

Oxley laughed out loud. He knew Colby had no intention of working. He had loaned him $500 already this morning. When both men glared at him he tried to cover up his blunder, but he didn't put much effort into it.

"Yeah man." He said. "We could certainly use a few dollars. The image of Colby working at Walmart isn't going to be a good look for us."

The knock at the door saved him.

Don Crawford, the Portland resistance leader who was being pushed out by Colby opened the door. Colby and Steve Oxley both recognized the smiling woman first. It was the singer and sometimes actress Eliana Kolnecik. And she was stunningly beautiful. While Colby didn't recognize either of the two men behind her, Oxley knew one of them.

It was Scotch Anderson. A thirty-something social media billionaire. Kolnecik walked directly to Colby and gave him a long hung. She was whispering into his ear words of love and encouragement.

Oxley shook hands with Anderson and the other man, who was holding a rather large backpack.

Anderson took charge of the meeting.

"Colby, we really think you're doing great work here. Really just great work. I could really use someone with your passion and drive to help run my business." He said. Then laughed and added,

"But you've got more important things to do I'm sure. Look, I know you look at us as the wealthy, evil capitalist, but we're not. We want the same things you want. But we have far less pull with the politicians and the bankers than you would think."

What Anderson and all of the other tech and media billionaires actually wanted was cheap labor and access to a billion Chinese to sell their products and movies too. But that wasn't really important right now. And Anderson figured Colby didn't need to know this.

"So the best way for us to help is with a little money. He looked to the man who had come with him and nodded.

The man started to speak, and Colby and Steve remained quiet, trying to figure out where this was going.

"We've made reservations at the Hilton downtown for your group. We have five large suites reserved for you through January. We also put a little gift pack together for you with some supplies and a few dollars for meals, clothes and anything else you might need."

The man handed the backpack to Colby and then gave him a card and a mobile phone. This is my card. I'm Mr. Anderson's personal assistant, so you call me if you need anything. This phone is for you as well. We think that your own cell phone might be bugged. This one is safer."

As he handed them the bag, Anderson spoke and his voice became a bit louder. Only Oxley noticed it.

He looked at his assistant as he spoke.

"Now, you didn't put anything bad in there, did you? Just some basic supplies and a few dollars like we agreed right?"

And he laughed as if it were some kind of inside joke. Colby laughed as well, not quite getting the joke. Oxley was dead silent and just stared at the bag.

Anderson stood up from the edge of the bed and the beautiful actress, who had been sitting close to Colby stood as well.

"Well, we're really pulling for you guys." Anderson said. And then he continued in a more serious note.

"Look Colby, if you need anything, be sure to get in touch with Sean here." He started to walk towards the door and then stopped again.

"Hey, one other thing guys. Call us if you need some guidance as well. We need the support of all the people. When you start to think the movement may be going off the rails and they start calling you a communist, let us help. And if you think that some of the crazier elements of your group want to overthrow the government, or get you into some real trouble, give us a call then as well. We can help you reel them back into sanity."

Oxley was silent, but Colby smiled and nodded like it was the best advice he had ever been given.

When they left Colby darted towards the backpack and started to fumble for the opening. But Steve stopped him.

"Wait a second Colby."

"What?"

"Don't you see what was going on here? They're trying to buy you off."

"Yeah, but that doesn't mean it will work." Colby retorted.

He went for the bag again, but Steve grabbed him by the shoulders and put his finger to his lips signaling Colby to be quiet.

Then he motioned him outside the door. Before he closed the door, he grabbed the new phone from Colby's hand and tossed it on the bed. When they were in the hallway he spoke quietly.

"That phone they gave you is probably the one that is bugged."
Colby had a confused look on his face. "What?"

"Think about what he said when his assistant handed you the bag. There is something in there that is illegal. Anderson was covering his ass in front of Elenia, and the phone is probably not just bugged when you talk, it's probably got a microphone in it to listen to everything we say. And that stuff he said at the end. He's trying to make sure you don't go too far and disrupt his business.

Whatever is in that backpack is either dangerous or a bribe. Let's just go to the Hilton and check-in. Just leave the phone behind. If they try to reach out again, tell them in all the excitement we forgot it."

Colby was beginning to understand. He nodded at Oxley and walked back into the room. He threw the backpack over his shoulder and said.

"All right Steve, things are starting to come together. We've got some dedicated voices in those guys who are willing to help us. Let's get out of this place and get to the Hilton and get to work."

When they had settled into all of their rooms Colby asked Oxley back to his room for a few minutes. Once alone he opened the bag. In the top of the bag were a few T-shirts. Underneath, there was money. Stacks and stacks of hundred dollar bills. They went layer by layer counting it.

"What are we at Steve?" Colby asked. The glee was overwhelming.

"Almost two hundred thousand dollars already, and there's still a layer to be counted." Oxley answered.
When Oxley reached in and pulled a few stacks from the last layer, he gasped.

"What the hell is it?" Colby asked.
Oxley picked up the bag and spread it open so Colby could see. At the bottom of the bag were four pistols. There were also a few boxes

of ammunition. Colby reached in and pulled out a folded piece of paper that was lying amongst the guns.

He opened it and read it aloud.

'Guys, I think it might get rough out there. You'll need to be able to protect yourself. I mentioned it to Scotch, but he thought it was too dangerous. I'm just worried about you. Please don't tell Scotch I put these in here, and be safe.'

Colby smiled and looked at Steve. Oxley was stunned.

"We have to get rid of these."

Colby shook his head no. "Steve, we already have guns. I gave two of them to Katana and I have two more in my bag."

"Why!" Oxley screamed. "What the hell do we need guns for?"

"Do you think the right wing guys that try to disrupt us don't have guns? They do. The guns are here to stop it from getting out of hand. We flash them to the right, they flash theirs to us. It's a way to prevent any of us from using them unless we absolutely have too.

Look, Steve, this is bigger than I think you realize. They aren't just going to walk away and let us run the country. It's going to take a fight. Without guns, they can just mow us down. People will be pissed for a few days, but then they'll forget all about us."

Oxley was nervous. "I thought you were against guns." He said.

Colby laughed heartily. "I'm against guns for the bad guys."

Colby flipped on the television and sat down on the couch in the living area of the suite.

The riots he had started were progressing as he had hoped. Smashed windows and burning cars were in every camera shot. The police had formed a wall. Colby could see they weren't holding a hard line. They would step back a few steps if the crowd surged.

There were the obligatory shots of young people with welts from rubber bullets and tear gas canisters being fired into the crowd. The crowd was huge. Much bigger than either Oxley or Colby could ever remember. Colby's mind was working quickly. Three of the others had joined him and Steve. Katana was still out in the streets stirring up the violence.

"I need you guys to do me a favor." Colby said. He reached into the bag and pulled out a few stacks of hundreds and threw them to Steve.

"Go out first thing tomorrow morning and buy a hundred tents. Big nice ones. Take them downtown and set them up like you are going to sleep in them. If anyone asks, tell them the tents are for everyone. Colby looked around the room at his four soldiers. That's what he needed them to be.

"You guys remember that Occupy Wall Street movement? Well, those guys hung on for months. We just need to hang on until the inauguration. When the tents fill up, give everyone inside a hundred dollars. Tell them we'll be back with more money."

"It will go fast if we give out too much." Steve said.
"No need to worry about that. Anderson may have covered his ass about the guns, but we've got him now. The guy is a billionaire. He'll give us as much as we need."

Just as Colby finished talking his phone buzzed. He grabbed and looked down at the caller id.

"It's Katy." He said and answered the phone. Katy was Katana. Katy was her real name and she hated it. But Colby knew this and would use it from time to time just to put her in her place. She was a loose cannon, so he needed to take every advantage he had to keep her in line.

"Katy, how's it going?"

"I've been arrested and the bond is a thousand dollars. I've got two hundred. Get your ass down here and get some money together to get me out!" She screamed.

"Where are you?"

"I'm in jail, you idiot!"

"I mean, where is the jail Katy?" He said with a condescending tone.

He sent all but Steve Oxley to bail her out. He handed Lee, the Asian kid, a stack of hundreds.

"Get her out and get her a lawyer. Use what's left to bail out any others you can afford."

When they left it was just he and Oxley again. Colby knew Oxley was nervous. He was worried it was going to be a big problem. But he also knew he needed him. He had a degree in history, and although he was the most contentious bastard he had ever met, he had a good relationship with him and the guy was usually right about things. So Colby wanted him calm and committed to the cause.

"Steve, I'm worried about you. You okay man?"

Oxley looked at him like he was crazy. "Damn Colby, are you kidding me? Aren't you worried this shit is getting out of hand? If someone gets killed tonight, this whole thing will be busted up and we'll all be in prison."

Colby tried to manage a smile. Steve was genuinely a nice guy. Those guys could be useful. But they were always afraid. That fear is what killed movements.

"Steve, Katana isn't down there to get someone killed. She is down there to make sure it doesn't happen."

This wasn't entirely true, Colby was just hoping no one would get killed. Not yet anyway. If it happened later, once they were solidified, then it happened. In a battle like this, there were sure to be deaths. It was part and parcel of the struggle

"Okay, I didn't know that about Katana. I thought she was there to stir shit up. But hell, now she's in jail. Colby, I gotta be honest. I think we want the same things. I mean we've always talked about it. National healthcare, more power for unions and working people, gun control and rights for women and minorities.

But this thing, I mean the way you are riling these people up, you're going to cause a civil war or some shit. And I don't want to be part of that. That won't end well for anyone. We can't win a war, Colby. We just can't. We have to stop this now."

Colby now knew that Oxley was a lost cause. This was the pivotal moment for Colby Ohlbinger. He knew this would happen. He was ready for it. He had prepared since he was a freshman in college eight years ago. He just thought it wouldn't happen so quickly.

But his moment would come tonight. He spent three hours talking to Oxley. Trying to calm him down and make him understand that he didn't want it to come to war. He didn't even want it to come to violence. A few broken windows were necessary he told him. That was all that was needed. A few broken windows a few cars on fire. Then people would see that they were serious.

They weren't going to have another election stolen from them. But he knew it wasn't working. He knew that something had to be done about Steve Oxley, and he knew he had to do it.

When Katana and the others finally returned to the hotel they were exhausted. The riots were all but over, but the people were still there.

Colby took Katana to her room and got her to sleep. She didn't need to be a part of what was going to happen. Oxley was too close and knew too much. If he ruined this, it would be forever. The nation would never get another chance. He had no idea if he could go through with his plan. But he knew it was the right thing to do.

He went back to his room. It was nearly two o'clock in the morning. "Steve, Lee, Jennifer, Manny, let's go for a walk." Colby said. Lee Jennifer and Manny stood quickly, but Steve sat still in his chair.

"Steve, I know you're tired, I just want to show you guys something. I just want to show you what you have accomplished tonight."

Steve reluctantly rose from his chair.
As they walked through the city, Colby talked.

He rambled on about how these people had been cheated their whole lives. Their parents and grandparents had good jobs and had made enough money to have a decent home and send their kids to college. He asked if any of them thought they would have enough money to send five kids to college.

He said that if any one of them got cancer, even if they had insurance and survived, they would be poor their entire lives. He kept walking and talking. A half hour passed and he found his spot. There was a small crowd. Thirty people at most. He blended in with them without talking to them. They were on the edge of the city. These people were clearly heading back to their cars or homes so Colby had to act fast.

The next moments would determine the outcome of his life and possibly the entire country. He was beginning to sweat and shake. Thoughts went back and forth in this mind. Did he believe in the cause enough to do what had to be done? He saw what he was looking for. A small alley between two old buildings that looked abandoned.

"Let's get out of here." He said as he ducked into the alley. All four followed.

The alley was narrow and short. At the end, it branched off into two other small alleys. Colby turned right as if he were going back to the hotel. After a few steps, he stopped.

He reached into his pocket and pulled one of the guns given to him by Anderson's assistant.

He put the gun to Steve Oxley's face and fired three times. Oxley slumped dead to the ground.

Jennifer, the youngest member of the group, screamed.

"Colby shoved the gun back into his pocket and covered her mouth.

Manny Gutierrez, the thin small Mexican raised his hands as if he were under arrest. Lee stood frozen and in shock.

"He was going to rat us out." Colby said quietly. "Steve was a plant. He was going to get us all thrown into prison. I told him I would go along with him to get you three arrested."

Jennifer fell silent. Colby knew he only had a few seconds. "Come with me."

Colby sprinted the opposite way back to the center of the city. At the end of the alley, he stopped.

"Split up, walk with a crowd and try to hold your shit together. Meet me back at my hotel room. Try to smile and laugh as much as you can. But don't stick out."

Colby ran off on his own. He was thankful when he got back to his hotel room that Manny had somehow beat him there. They both walked inside and waited. A few minutes later Lee knocked at the door.

Colby was aware that there were cameras in the hallway. So instead of letting him into the room he walked out into the hall and hugged Lee, laughed and smiled.

"We did it brother, what a great night!" While smiling and nodding he told Lee,

"Smile you dumb son of a bitch. You're on camera. He said it quietly, hoping the video didn't have audio. Lee smiled and looked around. Colby pulled him into the room.

"Sorry bud, I just didn't want you to get into trouble. If you looked nervous on that camera, the cops would be here and arrest you in minutes. Where's Jennifer?"

"I don't know." Was all the very young Lee Fong could manage to squeak out. He was terrified.

Colby walked him in and sat him down. He fixed him a soft drink and sat down next to him.

"Lee, I know this is rough, and if this ever comes out, I'll take the heat. But you have to understand, I did this for all four of us. Even Katana would have been in trouble. Steve was going to rat us out. I'm telling you."

Then Lee asked a question Colby hadn't considered. He was sure they would just go along.

"Rat us out for what?"

"For, well for, for... Steve thought we had caused all of the damage. He said it had gotten out of hand and each us was going to have to pay for all of the damage. He said we were trying to start a civil war and we would all go to prison for life. He was afraid. Steve was not a big believer in our cause. You guys know that. You have seen it with your own eyes. He was going to blame all of us. He was going to say he tried to stop it.

He tried to get me to go along with him, just like I said. He said we could get off the hook if we blamed you and Manny and Jennifer and Katana. The only reason I said I would was because it's not fair to you guys."

There was a soft knock at the door. As Colby opened the door, Jennifer came barreling in and threw herself on the floor sobbing.

Colby knelt beside her and calmly stroked her long black hair. She was so small. Colby had slept with her once. They were close, but she was just so awkward and shy. He told her what he had told Lee. How he had tried to save them and was willing to sacrifice himself if it came to that.

This made Jennifer even more frightened. Only now she was afraid for herself. She just wanted to go home.

"No!' Colby protested. You can't do that. We'll look guilty for killing Steve. Who knows who he talked to? We have to stick together. We have to go together for our rally tomorrow. Just like this morning. You guys have to sit behind me on the podium.

Lee, I need you. You're the organizational brains behind this. I want you to give a little speech. Guys, we have to stick together. Let's just get some sleep and see what happens in the morning. He prepared them for leaving his room.

He told them again about the cameras and how they had to act completely normal. They had to be laughing, and a few high fives would be great. Then, they were to stay in their rooms until ten AM, and come to his room.

They lingered much longer in the hallway than was necessary. Colby talked honestly about what they had accomplished. How they had brought people together and they were going to have their voices heard. Manny and Jennifer had actually loosened up a little and were feeling good.

Lee Fong couldn't figure out exactly how he had gotten himself into this mess. But he trusted Colby completely, so he went along with everything.

When he went back to his room, Colby immediately turned off the television. The last thing he heard was that shots had been fired, but police were suggesting it was probably unrelated to the protests, which other than a few broken windows and burnt out cars had been mostly peaceful.

He snapped off the TV, turned out the lights and laid in bed thinking. Killing Steve had been necessary. Not just because he wasn't on board, but because Colby knew all great leaders had to take command with violence.

He knew Manny, Lee or Jennifer would talk eventually. They would talk to other supporters of the cause. When they did this, it would earn him respect and fear. No one else would dare challenge him. He knew this would take time, but he knew it would happen.

What he didn't know was what he would do if he were caught by the police. This was the risk. If the police didn't immediately tie him to the crime, they never would. As word spread among the resistance that it was he who had killed Steve, the police would catch wind of this. But they would guess that it was just myth building on the part of Colby Ohlbinger created to hold power.

It would not occur to him that both things could be true. But if he were a suspect immediately, all would be lost. They would get Jennifer to break. And perhaps Lee as well. He thought about his friend Steve. He was nauseous. He had killed someone. He knew it had to be done. He had thought about it for years while planning his future. If a man wanted to lead a political revolution, people had to be killed.

He finally fell asleep. But the adrenaline still coursed through his body and he only slept for about four hours. At 7:30 in the morning he was wide awake with the television back on. The big story was still the protests. There had been a murder at the end of the night, but it appeared to be unrelated.

Another speech was scheduled for Three O'clock. Colby began to outline what he would say. At 8:00 his phone buzzed. It was a number he didn't know. It was a local reporter. She was just asking questions about the protests and where he thought they were going. She asked about his treatment of the mayor and the broken windows and other vandalism.

Colby said that letting off a little steam was to be expected. He again accused the politicians of selling them out and not standing for what was right. The calls continued from other local and national media. They were all identical. The narrative was being formed. He wondered who drove that. How was it that they all seemed to agree on the story?

After an hour or so the calls stopped for a few minutes, and he went back to his notes for the big speech. He would not report Steve Oxley missing. He would tell the others that he must have decided to return to Wisconsin.

His phone buzzed again. It was his contact from CNN. "This is Colby, how can I help you?" He answered.

"Colby, this is Jenks from CNN, are you sitting down?"

Colby's entire body convulsed in an instant. He knew this was going to be about Steve. Did CNN already know? Had something happened? He forced himself to be calm.

"I am now Donovan. You got me worried, what's happening?"

"Colby I hate to be the one to give you this news, but your friend Steve Oxley was murdered last night. I'm so sorry."

That was good. They didn't suspect him yet. He was silent for a long time. There was no need to say anything. He would let the reporter ask the questions.

"Colby, are you there buddy?"
"I'm here. I'm here. What? Are you sure? I mean, I went with him for a walk late last night. We kind of all split up and decided to head back home."

Shit! He shouldn't have offered anything. If the reporter talked to the police or mentioned that on the news they would be asking questions since he had seen him last.

"I'm sure Colby. I've got a source from the Portland PD. They said it's Oxley. They tracked him back to Wisconsin. They think it was a robbery gone bad. His wallet was in his pocket, but there was no money in it."

And another little piece of luck was in Colby's favor. Steve had no cash because Colby had borrowed every dime of it. But in a flash of brilliance, he decided to turn this into his advantage.

"Donovan, were his credit cards in his wallet. Because Steve didn't carry a lot of cash anyway."

"Oh, I don't know Colby."

"Oh my God. I just, I'm sorry, this is just awful. Steve was, Steve was really the brains behind our little group. The guy was just the best. Thank you for the call, Donovan. I really appreciate it. I've got too... I guess I've got to tell the others. I feel like I'm going to throw up. I'm just. I gotta go Donovan."

Colby hung up the phone without saying goodbye. He hoped his performance had worked.

He threw away the paper with the speech he had been writing and started over. He knew what he was going to say.

At three, as scheduled he approached the podium. The news of Steve Oxley's death had not spread. He had his four soldiers seated behind him and the local leaders as well. He made sure to leave one seat empty in memory of Steve Oxley. In one brilliant move, he would solidify his control and make sure the police never dared look in his direction.

He ambled to the microphone his head down. The crowd was already yelling slogans. The quiet and respect he had earned yesterday already gone. He shook his head unconsciously at how fickle they could be. The group, misinterpreting the gesture, cheered even louder.

A feminist with her own megaphone was trying to get the crowd to her side. An immigrant with a Mexican flag was screaming for amnesty and citizenship. A black woman was screaming about police brutality. It was a mix of too many groups to count.

Colby had worked madly for the last hour before his speech by himself. He finally found the shirt he was looking for and was wearing it underneath his coat. He slowly and deliberately unzipped his coat revealing a Chicago White Sox jersey underneath. The crowd had grown silent.

He simply pointed to the word "SOX" on the front of his shirt. He then backed away from the microphone and towards the crowd so everyone could see it.

He said nothing, but twisted his face to pretend as if he were trying with all his strength to stop from crying. Then he walked back to the empty seat and sat.

The crowd and the media were both confused. Only Donovan Jenkins of CNN knew what was going on. He talked to his producer frantically.

"Keep the camera on him, keep it on him and zoom in."

The shot was perfect. Colby lowered his head and covered his face. He shook his shoulders to fake crying. The crowd was now completely silent. He stood and walked to the microphone.

"Most of you don't know what this shirt means do you? Well, I'm going to tell you exactly what it means." He thundered.

"Sox! Sox was the man sitting in that chair yesterday. His name was Steve Oxley. He was such a passionate supporter of our cause. He was my strength. He was no coward. Sox was a fighter.

This morning I got a call from a good friend with a connection to the Portland Police Department. Steve Oxley was murdered in cold blood last night. Gunned down!

The police are going to tell you that Steve Oxley was murdered in an attempted robbery. They said his wallet had no cash in it. Those of us who knew Sox know that he never carried cash!

And I have also found out that Steve Oxley's credit cards weren't taken!"

It would not be questioned how Colby knew this. But it was of course true. Donovan figured he did have a source in the Portland PD, as did everyone else.

"Steve Oxley wasn't murdered in an attempted robbery. Steve Oxley was murdered either by one of two groups. The Portland police or the right wing infiltrators!"

The crowd was now furious. Colby knew he had momentarily lost control. There was no sense in trying to get it back. They didn't know Steve Oxley at all. But they knew he was one of them and had been murdered. Lee would not get to give his speech. As Colby noticed the crowd starting to slowly disperse to vent their rage he started his own chant.

"Sox! Sox! Sox!"

Others joined the chant and stood to wait for more of the speech. But most joined the crowd in its exodus to destruction.

Colby joined the media to give his sad and somber interviews. He was now in control not just of the Madison Wisconsin resistance. Not just of the Portland Oregon resistance, but of the national resistance.

The police, having now been accused, could not even interview him as the last person who had seen him alive.

His last victory of the day had been a personal appeal to Scotch Anderson, though he never mentioned the name. He said during an interview that there had been some very wealthy benefactors who had donated money to him and his group. He wanted to thank them for their support. The money was now gone, sent to Steve Oxley's parents. He did not want to beg, but he needed more help.

Ohlbinger had sent ten thousand dollars to Oxley's parents. The next morning three backpacks with more than a million dollars stuffed in them showed up at his door. The money would continue. Later that night Colby started to think about Steve. He wanted to cry. He wanted to go home. Why had he done it? He thought about the things he wanted to accomplish. He thought about the money he had. He could do it. He could succeed. If he kept focused he would change the country.

He tried to tell himself that Steve would have ruined everything. He felt that in some small way he was right. Steve was going to break. He was from a wealthy family. His father would have gotten to him. For Steve Oxley, this was a cause, but also something to do. He was not committed. There was no option.

There were going to be tough days ahead. Colby knew this. He may have to kill again. He knew this as well. But he would never do it face to face and up close. And he would never kill one of his own again.

CHAPTER 4

JANUARY: THE EARLY BATTLES

T he second inauguration was stopped immediately after President Johnson's speech. The crowd was mixed with supporters and protestors shoving, pushing and a few fist fights had broken out.

The President was determined to make the traditional drive through the city. He had been warned that he could not leave the limousine. He had negotiated with the Secret Service to lower the window and wave to the crowd. The drive had not lasted five minutes when the first piece of fruit splattered along the side of the presidential limousine. Within seconds the entire motorcade was pelted with coins, fruit and small rocks.

The agents guarding the motorcade pulled their guns and advanced on the crowd. They were overwhelmed. Although no weapons had made it into the crowd, the fights were violent and many were injured. The start of Bill Johnson's second term was not going well.

In the early evening just ten days later Johnson had called a meeting. It was supposed to be a small affair with the party leaders in the House and Senate to discuss the economy. But all eyes had been glued to the television.

The violence in Indianapolis was growing. This was unexpected. Other cities were experiencing protests and riots. But in Indianapolis, it had turned bloody. In Portland Oregon, it was clear that the protestors were in charge of the city. All across the nation, the resistance protestors raged.

Bond prices were rising by the day, and so was unemployment. The Feds second attempt at quantitative easing and printing money was failing, and Johnson was getting the blame.

The Republicans were sure they needed to cut spending and the Democrats were angry that the Republicans were even in charge.

"That lunatic in Portland Oregon has got the Democrats frozen." Someone offered. The president nodded absently just watching the television. The slight majority the Democrats had in the House meant no spending cuts were going to get through anyway.

"What's that guy's name?" Someone else asked.

"Ohlbinger. He's some young college professor or something I can't recall. Hell, he's on CNN and MSNBC every other day. From what we're hearing he is actually running the city of Portland. They don't dare make a move without him. Now there are even wild rumors that he killed one of his own lieutenants just to keep everyone in line. Local PD says it was just a robbery gone bad, but who knows. Well, they'll all flame out in a couple of days anyway. What is our plan on the economy Mr. President?"

The president pulled himself from the television but before he could answer Victor Van Driessen spoke up. He wasn't supposed to be here. But at the last minute, the President had invited him personally.

"No. I don't think this is going to fade away. Not this time."

"What makes you say that Vic?" The President asked.

"Because the crowds have been growing not shrinking. And look at some of the people in the crowd. In the past, they have either been mostly black, Hispanic, or young white men and women. They were kids really. And they were protesting for their own issues.

This crowd really is mixed. And there are men and women in their thirties and forties in the crowd. And it's the same in other cities. The numbers are growing, and the rhetoric is becoming more violent. Nothing is held back."

"I noticed that as well." The President said.
"This economy is hurting people. Too many are losing their jobs and homes."

"Van Driessen is right." Vice-President Hoxworth added. "But as soon as the mob realizes what these socialists are actually after I think most of them might fall out."

"Some of them. But most will probably stay. The younger people don't have much hope of finding a job right now. So they'll just hang out. The people in their thirties and forties are frustrated and ready to lash out. The kids aren't going back to college and too many of the adults don't have jobs to go back to. " Van Driessen answered.

Just as they were to sit down and discuss plans to stimulate the economy someone shouted, "Oh my God!" and the entire group turned to the television.

The reporter and cameraman were backpedaling and trying to show the scene at the same time. There were bodies lying all over the street. Gunshots could still be heard but they were sporadic.

The reporter was struggling to tell the story. The protestors had been attacked. They were unsure of the details but they had heard gunfire and seen people falling.

The reporter said that he had to sign off for a moment to get to safety and the feed returned to the anchor desk.

"Well, clearly there has been some kind of right-wing attack on these protestors, who were for the most part peaceful. Isn't that what you take from this John?"

The young woman looked to the older anchor for assistance. "It does look that way Angela, but we really don't know for sure."

The President flipped through channels looking for more information. He called the head of the NSA, but they had no better information than the news channels.

Only a few minutes passed and the press secretary was already calling President Johnson for a statement. He told her to put them off for an hour and hung up the phone.

He turned back to the news and raised his hand to silence the room.

They were going back to the scene where the reporter had a witness to what had happened. The reporter was holding the microphone and told the anchors that they had a witness, and perhaps participant in the violence that had taken place.

Standing next to her was a tall thin white man with short blonde hair. An AK47 rifle was slung over his shoulder. He was neatly dressed, clean shaven and had bright blue eyes.

"Sir, you say you were in the middle of this violence. I see you have a gun as well. Can you tell us what is your name and what transpired here?"

"Uh, yes ma'am. My name is Tanner Ritchie. I'm from Missouri and I've been up here in Indianapolis with a few friends. We were staying in a hotel downtown and realized we couldn't get out safely. So we grabbed our guns and decided to just make a run for it and head out of the city to get back home.

We had brought the guns to go shooting with a cousin of mine who lives outside of town. And well, we didn't get far and it was just chaos."

"Okay, so did you witness these people being shot?" The reporter asked.

"Oh yes mam. I shot a few of them myself. Like I said, we were just trying to get out of the city and we walked through the crowd. And they, the protestors I mean, started throwing rocks and bottles at us. We leveled our guns in self-defense and that's when someone fired on us.

None of us were hit luckily. But yes Ma'am. We returned fire pretty quickly to try to escape." He stopped talking and smiled broadly.

"I know what you're thinking, but no. We didn't attack anyone. The crowd was after us, I guess because we're white, I don't really know. But we had no choice."

"Sir, do you mean that you killed all of these people?"
"Oh, I didn't know some had died. We tried to fire low at their feet just to scare them off and maybe hit them in the legs.

Well, that's a shame. I'm...gosh, I didn't know that some had died. But this is clearly a war now. And I'm hoping that some other patriots that love America will come and help us out.

I'm sure the police in a big city like this are pretty liberal and we're going to be in big trouble. So if any good Americans who believe in the second amendment are out there I hope they get to Indianapolis soon.

We're planning on meeting up on the south side of the city and hopefully they can help get us out of this mess. Otherwise, I'm pretty sure they'll pin this on us like we are murderers. But I promise you ma'am. We were just trying to get out of here when we were attacked."

The reporter, now visibly frightened looked back to the camera. She needed to hand this story off and get out of Indianapolis. She hoped the anchor team wouldn't ask her any questions.

They didn't. But her producers were furious. The man had just asked for more people to come into the city and bring guns, and it had been broadcast all across the country. They knew something wasn't right.

Tanner Ritchie stood still, waiting to see if there were more questions coming. He was professional, intelligent, and very friendly. Tanner Ritchie was also a psychopath.

The only part of his story that was true was that he was from Missouri. He and three other friends had come to Indiana to start a war. When his interview was over, he ran to a predetermined meeting place far outside of the city. He knew the police would be looking for him.

Three interstate highways feed into the south side of Indianapolis. I-70, I-65, and I-74. Tanner and his three friends would just drive between the exits of these highways and the 465 loop that surrounded the city. If they saw a small group, they would meet up with them and form their army.

If not, they could escape back to Missouri. That was the plan. But Tanner had no intention of sticking to that plan. If no one showed, he would hide out and take a second run at the protestors. He was however not to be disappointed.

The next morning Tanner had found his supporters. Hundreds of them. They were mad, well-armed and ready to fight. By afternoon they had put together a plan.

They would slowly ease into the city in small groups. Then meet up downtown when it was dark. Seven O'clock was to be the hour. They would patrol the streets as liberators. Anyone who tried to stop them had to be dealt with.

As the day wore on, all of the networks were reporting that in fact, Tanner Ritchie and his group were the aggressors.

Witnesses with blurry phone video showed a raucous crowd, but one that wasn't violent. Then suddenly dozens were mown down in a hail of gunfire. But trust in the media was at an all-time low and many did not believe the story.

Tanner seemed to be a polite, friendly boy who would never have done something like that.

The next night was peaceful. After the previous night's massacre, no protestors showed. Many of the new arrivals were interviewed. They were ask if they were supporting Tanner, white nationalism, or some other right-wing cause.

The interviewees gave several different reasons. But none would say where Ritchie was. Most suggested he had left. But Tanner was in the group. His hair now died black, a baseball hat and a five-O'clock shadow was disguise enough for the night.

For two days they patrolled the city. The police left them alone, afraid of causing further violence. By the third night, all were on edge.

From Portland, Colby Ohlbinger had given an interview on the massacre. He had encouraged his supporters not to give up. This massacre was designed to put the young, the minorities, and the disadvantaged back in their place. He had said.

And it was working. They were being scared into passive acceptance once again. They needed to fight back.

That night, the left wing groups showed they weren't going to go quietly this time. The resistance would finally resist.

The trouble started just as darkness had fallen. For two hours there had been screaming and throwing of bottles and rocks. The police had cordoned off several blocks. But no shots were fired.

Tanner Ritchie was growing frustrated. His army was not stopping the protesters. He knew there were cameras everywhere. The police were boxing the crowd in closer and closer. He had to act. He slunk back behind the corner of a building where it was dark.

A large concrete plant stand was just to his left. He had cover. He had left his rifle in the car so he pulled out a pistol. A .22 caliber with a ten shot capacity. He fired three rounds quickly into the crowd and hid the gun in his pocket.

The crowd started to disperse quickly. But unlike his first attack, this time there was return fire.

The massive second slaughter he envisioned did not materialize. The first return shots had hit four of his "Rebel" army. Most scattered quickly. Some returned fire.

For several minutes this is the way it went. Short bursts of fire back and forth as both sides took up defensive positions.

The rest of the night was quieter. Occasionally a shot or two would ring out. The police were unable to get any control of the situation. They had no idea who had guns, how many they had, or where they were.

But the fighters on both sides were also afraid.
The media, right in the middle of it until the first shots, had pulled back to the edge of the city. No one was sure what was going on and no one knew how it would end.

For three days it went like this. But slowly, the tens of thousands who had come to join the resistance protest started to gain an advantage. Tanner Ritchie's forces were dwindling quickly.

The resistance, as they had termed themselves years ago, grew in numbers. On a Friday night they would make their move. Three groups of a few hundred each, stayed together and swept the city.

There were deaths on both sides, but the Rebels, as recently designated by Ritchie, took the brunt of the attacks and fell apart.

Most that were left escaped, regrouping at I-70 well outside the city. But a few were left behind. By Saturday night they had been captured by the resistance. They were paraded through the streets tied together with rope. There were just five men, but they were a powerful symbol.

John Hartwick sat at home watching television. His wife Audrey watched nervously from the kitchen.

They were in a friendly, upper middle-class, suburban area, and well outside of the city. Hartwick felt safe, but Audrey wasn't so sure.

She was also nervous about money. No one in the city had worked for ten days. It was early in the year, but John's company had allowed everyone to take an extra weeks' vacation early. That would help. But for how long?

Hartwick had left Ohio right out of college. For almost ten years he had enjoyed a great life in San Jose California. The pay was great, but the cost of living was high. Still, they had done well enough.

At thirty, he had been promoted to a team lead. The money was even better. One hundred and fifty-thousand per year even in San Jose was not bad.

And then it had all fallen apart. The tech startup had lost funding and folded. He found another job quickly. The money was a bit less but still not bad. The bigger problem was that he had lost his promotion track. Now he was writing code again. Work he enjoyed even if the pay was lower.

And then it fell apart again. The company had decided to outsource some of the work to a company in India. They also brought in fifty H1b Visa programmers. Hartwick was out of a job again.

This time he couldn't find another that paid enough to live in San Jose with a wife and two kids.

He left for a job in Indianapolis. The pay was half what he had made in San Jose. But he had a bigger house and actually a better life. They had finally adjusted.

In just two years he had already been promoted. Now at thirty-eight-years-old he thought he might be out of a job again. There had been rumors that the company was going to move to Texas.

Audrey didn't want to go because the kids were in elementary school. And both of their parents lived fairly close. But if this kept up for another week, he would have to make a decision. Their savings wouldn't hold out for long. And with the economy tanking, he thought he might not get a job at all.

As he watched the live news coming from Indianapolis he started to seethe. At first, he was mad at the lunatics who had broken up the protest with a mass murder.

The protests had been like so many others. A few broken windows, stopped traffic for a few days and then they left and everything went back to normal. This time things were different.

The protestors had taken control and were marching five men down the middle of the street. The story from the media was that these five men had been with Tanner Ritchie. They were the ones who had committed the massacre.

There was no single leader among the resistance. Just a group of leaders of smaller groups. As soon as they had captured the rebels, their first move was to call Colby Ohlbinger.

Colby had just landed back in Portland. He had flown first class. As he picked up his bag and headed back to the hotel he was preoccupied with how easy it had all been.

The entire nation knew he had led the protests, and was probably behind the violence. Yet he had boarded a plane, flown halfway across the country to give a speech rallying other protesters in Madison Wi, met with some people in Indianapolis, Columbus and Cincinnati, and flew all the way back to Portland. No one had said a word or tried to stop him. He was smiling to himself when the phone buzzed.

"Ohlbinger, how can I help you?" He answered.

"Colby, hey man, don't know if you remember me but we talked on the phone yesterday. I'm in Indianapolis. My name's Zach Hale. We caught the guys that did the massacre. We got them right now. What should we do?"

Ohlbinger was trying to suppress his jubilation. The fact that they had called him confirmed, at least in his own mind, his position as the leader of the resistance. But he had to be calm. The letter in the bag from Scotch Anderson's assistance flashed in his mind.

That had been a brilliant way to distance himself from any crime. He had to do the same. This was not like before. These guys were not Steve Oxley, they were murders and they were the enemy.

"Are the police around?" He asked.

"Naw brother, they pulled way back. We're running the show down here. Just like you said man. What should we do with them?"

"Now, are you sure these are the guys?" Colby asked.
"Yeah, ummm, we're pretty sure dude. They were definitely with the group and they had guns."

"Okay, well, this is a big moment for you guys. But you want to keep it safe. Is anyone calling for you to kill the guys?"

"Well, they want blood, so yeah, I guess so."
This was what Colby was looking for.

"Okay. This is going to sound strange. But if you want to stay in control Zach, you're going to have to give them what they want. I know this is hard, but these guys, they're cold-blooded killers. They would probably get the death penalty if you turned them over to the police. But the crowd might not like that. You know what I mean."

"Yeah, I was thinking the same thing." Hale answered.
"Alright then Zach. Are you my guy in Indianapolis? I mean can I count on you to join the nationwide leadership?"

"Absolutely sir."

Sir. He had said sir. Colby noticed the change in respect and deference and was quiet for a second.

"You're going to have to get someone to line them up and shoot them. But before you do it, you need to make sure everyone can hear you. So get a megaphone and tell the crowd the guys confessed."

"Yeah, but they really didn't conf.."
Colby cut him off quickly.

"If you don't think you can pull the trigger, and that's fine Zach, get a couple of the wild ones from the group. But try to make sure they are cool and calm. Tell them about the confession and what needs to be done. Can I count on you Zach? And hey, if this leadership position isn't for you it's cool. It doesn't mean you're a coward or anything. Really, I understand. But this is important. So is there someone else there I need to talk to?"

The challenge was clear. Both men knew it. "No, no I got this. I'll get it done and call ya back okay?"

Colby ended the call immediately. He had heard what he wanted to hear.

Hartwick was watching it all unfold live. The men had been forced to sit down in the center of the road. There were bottles thrown at them and occasionally someone would kick them.

Someone stepped forward and pulled on the rope for them to stand. He then marched them towards the sidewalk out of the street and against a building. The man grabbed a megaphone.

A group of three more joined him. All had rifles slung over their shoulders.

The man with the megaphone started speaking.

"These men are responsible for the murders of our friends. These men killed seventeen people in cold blood!"

The crowd was screaming. The noise was so loud the reporter couldn't even be heard.

The sentence was carried out quickly. Zachary Hale, college dropout, full-time protestor, and part-time graphic designer dropped the megaphone, pulled a handgun from his coat pocket, turned with the other three men, and executed the five accused murderers.

"Holy shit. What the fuck!" John Hartwick screamed at his television.

"What John? What happened?" His wife asked.

"They just executed five guys. They said they were the ones who had killed the people earlier this week."

Hartwick stared at his wife in silence. There were tears in her eyes. She instinctively called the kids in from the backyard where they were playing.

"I have to go. I have to do something." Hartwick said.

"No John, you can't go down there." Audrey protested.

"I'm not. I'm going to I-70 and 465. I just want to see if other people have had it with this. Something has to be done Audrey. These people are insane. All of them. Normal people have to do something. Where the hell are the police?"

Hartwick pulled off the exit and into a huge parking lot where all the big box stores were. He was stunned at how many people were standing around talking.

It was cold and he had his big gray North Face coat on. In the right pocket was his gun and in the left a box of .38 caliber bullets. He felt a bit foolish now for taking it. He had calmed down on the drive. He didn't know what would happen, but he knew something had to be done.

There were some rough looking men in the crowd of about a thousand people. But most were like himself. Well dressed and groomed, with coats and gloves. He parked his car and walked towards an area where a group of thirty or forty had gathered. A younger man, tall with black hair was talking.

"We've got to get back in there. We have to take the city back. Run those fucking socialists out."

Most of the men were just listening. A few nodded in agreement. John Hartwick wanted no part of this. He knew there were thousands, maybe tens of thousands in the city. He decided to speak up. He had to find out where this crowd really was. If they were hell-bent on a gunfight he would just leave.

"Seems to me the best option is to just close them in. Don't let anyone in and don't let any trucks past 465. They'll get hungry and the out of town trouble makers will leave." He offered.

"Fuck that. They'll just come back. We have to go in there and either wipe them out or load them up and ship them out to California where they belong!"

The younger man retorted.

"I don't know." Hartwick said. "We've got maybe a thousand or so here. We could win, but just like those other guys, a lot of us would get killed. Why don't we just trap them in there?"

"How?" Another man asked.

"We just need to block the major highways. Stop them from getting past 465. Then we slowly pinch closer to the suburbs to help those folks, but close off the city. Stop them from getting food. When we get close enough, shut off the electric and cut the phone lines, or the cell towers or whatever we need to do.

But, let them leave. Let them go back to Chicago or wherever the hell else they came from." Hartwick said.

"That sounds like a better plan." The other man said. Pretty soon most of the crowd was agreeing with John. But the dark-haired, younger man was belligerent and would not budge. The small crowd quickly grew to listen to the debate. When it became clear that most of the crowd agreed with Hartwick the young man blew up.

"Fuck you guys. I came here to fight. I started this shit and now you guys want to fucking just stand around until they get tired. Then what? Yeah, they might leave for a while but they'll be back. Fuck it. I'm going back to Missouri to be with my own people."

And with that, he walked to a nearby truck, jumped in and sped off.

"Who the hell was that guy?" Hartwick asked.

"I think it was that Tanner Ritchie. The guy on TV that said he and his group killed all of those people last week."

Hartwick just shook his head. "Sheesh. I don't think some of these folks are right in the head."

He started to talk about the containment plan. Someone had a pen and a notepad and they counted people, and figured out how many could be at each highway. And then someone was yelling. The group turned to see two men running from their cars towards them. "They're attacking the sporting goods store!"

When they got closer they were able to talk. A large group, over a hundred, was attacking a sporting goods store the next exit up. They were trying to take all of the guns. Someone looked at Hartwick.

"We gotta stop this don't we?"

"Is it that Tanner Ritchie and his group?" Hartwick asked.

"No, it's the protesters from the city. The left wingers."

"Yeah, I think we need to stop this." Hartwick said.

Hartwick screamed out orders. He had no idea how he had ended up in this position. Perhaps it was just luck he figured. He'd spoken up against Tanner Ritchie and that had earned him at least a temporary leadership position. He told them to get there fast and make sure they didn't get out with those guns. He was determined to end this occupation of Indianapolis so he could get back to work and feed his family. He vowed he wouldn't be moved around the country a third time.

He jumped in the front passenger seat of an SUV with a few other men he did not know. They introduced themselves on the ride to the sporting goods store.

They could see the chaos even before they got off the exit. People were running out of the stores with rifles in their hands, and bags that they guessed were ammunition.

They were all running away from the store towards the back of the parking lot where several dozen cars were parked haphazardly.

"Stop here!" Hartwick screamed. "We can look down on them from the overpass and stop them."

Others ahead of them were already pulling into the lot. The rest soon understood the plan.

John ran as fast as he could with his pistol in his hand, yelling at the resistance group to stop. He yelled that they were surrounded.

He heard a shot and felt a bullet whizz past his head. He fell to the ground to take cover.

He was laying on the ground trying to fumble for his pistol that he had dropped. He realized it wasn't even loaded. But as he reached for the bullets in his other pocket the sound of gunfire became deafening. All around him the men he had come with were firing into the group below.

He stopped trying to load his gun and slowly raised his head to witness the carnage. Bodies were dropping everywhere. The people stealing the guns had not bothered to stop and load them. John saw no return fire at all.

After a few long minutes, he could hear people yelling 'cease-fire'. Finally, all was quiet. A few lone people in the parking lot below stood slowly with their hands raised high.

John stood up and made his way down the hill into the parking lot. After just a couple of steps, he looked behind.

Most of the men were following. Their guns were still aimed. John became aware of how fast and hard his heart was beating. His entire body was slick with sweat and he was shaking violently. He had never been more terrified.

As he walked, he started to calm down. He kept his eyes on the people with their hands raised. They were completely still. All around them lay the dead and dying.

As others started to get closer John held his right hand up. "Get these guys into the back of a truck. Do we have anything to tie their hands?"

"We should line them up and shoot them. Just like they did our guys." One of the men said.

John turned to see who had said it. A burly six foot four man with a full beard and his gun over his shoulder walked up to Hartwick.

"Don't you think they deserve it?"

"I don't know. Probably. But do we really want to be like them?"

"I'm an electrician. Someone else said. I got cable ties in my van. I'll use those as handcuffs. Where are we going to take them?"

John was happy that the brief tense moment was diffused. "I don't know, let's just take them back to the parking lot we came from for now." He said.

The burly man just shrugged. "Well, at least gather up all of these guns and take them too. It's looking like we're going to need them."

Hartwick had a clear but somewhat disturbing thought. He looked at the big man. "What about the rest of them in that store?" Hartwick asked.

"You mean steal them all?" He said.

"Well, if we don't, aren't we risking another attack like this? I don't want them to get the guns."

"Take 'em all boys. Go into the store and get every gun and every bit of ammunition and bring it back to our rally point."

The burly man, Jake Stahl was his name, walked off towards the store. A few other men grabbed the resistance fighters who had not been wounded and quickly led them up the hill towards the highway and into the back of a truck.

Just moments later police cars started to pull into the parking lot. A small crowd had gathered and Hartwick found himself at the center of attention again.

Some of Hartwick's group were tending to the wounded. The scene was calm but the police quickly jumped out of their cars with guns drawn.

Hartwick raised his hands, as did most of the others. "Whoah, whoah. We were the ones attacked." He protested.

"Keep your hands up and those of you with guns drop them and raise your hands!"

The thirty or so men did as told. But a voice from up on the hill yelled out.

"Officer you better drop your guns. You are surrounded by about five-thousand guns aimed at you and those men are with us and we were attacked!"

All of the officers heard this and started scanning the surrounding area. There were men and guns aimed from everywhere. A long moment passed and no one said a word as the tension built. Hartwick walked slowly towards the police with his hands raised.

"Easy officer, easy. I'm just trying to diffuse this."

He could see the policemen tense up but they said nothing. He turned and yelled up towards the hill. "Easy boys. I'm just going to talk to the officers here and explain what happened."

An older officer walked from the back. He would pat the other police on the back as we walked past them towards Hartwick. "Stand down guys. This is a fight we don't want."

He walked up to Hartwick and motioned for John to put his hands down. Both men were trying to remain calm. "What happened here?"

The gray-haired cop said, as he waved his arm towards the bodies.

"Well sir, we were meeting just up the road. We're just a group of men that are sick of what is going on in the city. We need to get back to work. So we were talking about what we could do and someone came running up and told us a bunch of the protesters were up here stealing guns.

So we jumped in our cars and raced here to stop them. When we got here I came down the hill from the overpass, me and a couple of others, and tried to get them to stop. And they shot at us.

Then all hell broke loose and our guys started firing back." The older officer nodded as if he understood. "What's your name son?"

"I'm John Hartwick."

"I'm Captain Duane Andrews." He reached out his hand to shake John's hands. One of them men behind John reached down for his gun and another officer drew on him and screamed.

"Stay where you are sir!"

A single shot rang out from the hills. Everyone froze. Incredibly, no other shots followed.

Captain Andrews turned to the cop who had drawn his weapon. "Son, what in the absolute hell are you doing?"

John turned to the man who had tried to pick up his gun. "Easy man, just leave it there for a second.

Andrews moved his officers back a bit. "All right guys. Let's all calm down. Lower your weapons."

As he talked he walked the police back towards their cars and then turned back to Hartwick.

"Son, none of us want a battle here. But I can't just let you leave, can I? I mean, I don't know. Let me get the Chief or maybe the Sheriff on the radio here, and find out what they want me to do. Is that okay?"

Hartwick just shrugged his shoulders. Andrews leaned his head over into the microphone on his right and pressed the button. "This is Captain Andrews, can you get the chief for me?"

"He's right here."

The talk was brief. Andrews told the chief what had transpired and asked for direction. Hartwick heard the answer. "Just arrest the leaders and bring them in for questioning."

Andrews looked at Hartwick. John just shook his head back and forth.

"No. I don't think we're going to be able to do that Chief. We're outnumbered about twenty to one. Sir, I think the best option here is to help with the squads and get the wounded and dead out. I'll hang out and talk to the leaders and take it from there. Good enough?"

"I can call other forces in if you need Duane." The chief responded.

"No, let's not make this worse. I'll fill you in when I get back."

When he ended the conversation he asked Hartwick. "That fair enough? You give me the real story and we back out? I don't want this to get worse, and I don't think you do either."

"No sir I don't." Hartwick answered.

The police helped load the ambulances. They had kept the reporters out for now. Hartwick's group on the perimeter held their positions.

Jake Stahl, the big bearded man, had quietly emptied hundreds of guns and all the ammunition he could from the store.

But they weren't able to get nearly all of it. As the police started moving closer to the store, Jake and a few others quietly loaded up a few dozen trucks on the highway and went back to the original shopping center.

"So what can you tell me about all this?" Andrews asked Hartwick.

"It's just what I told you. After I saw those protesters murder the guys on live TV I came up here. Everyone knew that the rebel group had gathered around here initially.

Then we heard about this, and we all came to stop it."

"So are you part of that so-called rebel army?"

"No. I mean, I don't think so." Hartwick chuckled. "Look, we just need to get back to work. There are a couple of rough ones with us, but for the most part, it's just us guys that live in the suburbs or rural areas around here that want to get things back to normal."

"So what's your plan?"

Hartwick told him about the plan to surround the city and starve them out. They wouldn't let anyone in, only out. They figured in a week or two the protestors would get hungry, or tied of living in tents and leave.

"Problem you got there is that they've taken over the hotels. So they may be able to hold out a bit longer than you think." Andrews offered.

"But, I gotta be honest, it's a better plan than going in there with guns blazing trying to drive them out. But what do you think all of the local police and Sheriff's deputies are going to do when you shut down 465? There are quite a lot of people in those little cities and suburbs close to the cities. What about them?"

John sensed that this was a pivotal moment. If he could get the police to help them, or at least leave them alone, things would move quicker and he could get back to work.

"We really haven't thought that far ahead I guess. We were just kind of putting the plan together when all hell broke loose here."

Andrews took out a business card. He wrote something on the back of it.

"This is my card. Try me first on my police phone. If you can't reach me there, the numbers on the back are my personal phone and my home phone. Call me tonight. I'll go back and talk to the chief. Then we can call the local PDs and sheriff's offices around the outside of the city.

I don't know what they'll say. But in my mind, it's a hell of a lot better idea than anything else I've heard. Sound like a plan?"

Hartwick nodded and took the card.

When the chaos had settled and the men were back at the shopping center, Hartwick had a quiet moment. He realized that nothing was going to go as planned. But at least they had one.

A reporter was walking around trying to interview people. But they all kept sending him to John Hartwick. John was sitting on the back bed of a pickup truck. Talking to a reporter in front of a camera. He explained what had happened but the reporter kept insisting he was part of the rebel army.

"Look, you keep saying that. But there is no rebel army. We're just a group of guys that want things back to normal. These protesters can't keep disrupting our lives and trying to force things on us we don't want.

I've lost two jobs because of legal immigration. These politicians and big businesses for years kept sending manufacturing jobs to China, Mexico and who knows where else. We were told that this was good for the economy. That these trade deals would allow Mexico to do better and people wouldn't run across the border. That didn't work, did it?

Then they told us we can ship all these jobs to China and the stuff we would buy would be cheaper.

Well, it is cheaper I guess. But we have to pay more taxes because people are making less money here. So that didn't work. Then, they started bringing immigrants in and taking jobs or lowering the salaries of the white collar workers. They leave the border wide open and more immigrants come in illegally.

But if we suggest that this may not be good for us, people on television tell everyone we are a bunch of racists or bigots. I get it. The people coming into this country want a better life. But what about the people who are already here? When do get a break? When do we get a chance to catch our breath and build a little something for our future?

Look, I said nothing for years. Because it didn't affect me. I should have spoken up. And so should all the other people like me.

But we didn't. And now that we have all been affected we still didn't say anything. We didn't riot or protest.

But because an election didn't go the way some people wanted, they protest and shut down cities and make things even worse. I'm not going to shut up anymore. I didn't want this to happen. All we wanted was for the protesters to leave. That's it.

And then we found out that they were raiding a gun store! We had to stop it. If they had stolen hundreds of guns we may have never been able to return to work. We just want to work, earn a decent salary, and be left alone."

"But sir, don't you realize that the protesters want the same thing? They want a livable minimum wage, a fair national health care system so no one is left bankrupt and, for many of the younger more educated protesters, not to be in debt from college before starting their lives. Don't you really want the same thing?"

The report asked. The condescension in her tone fairly obvious.

"How? How do they plan to pay for all of this? How is this supposed to work?" Hartwick said.

The reporter, not expecting to be asked a question, turned away from John and towards the camera. "So there you have it. It looks like the protesters and the rebels will continue to disagree. But hopefully, they will both be smart enough to stop the violence."

By the next day the interview had been shown by all the cable news networks several times. The media were starting to understand that this was more than protests and that things were getting out of hand.

Hartwick and his group settled in for the siege. Every major highway exit into the city had at least three hundred armed men stopping traffic from going in.

Every couple of days they would let a truck delivering food or medicine pass.

There was nothing to do but wait. The police had agreed to let them alone. Most of the politicians had left. Indianapolis, as the capital of the state of Indiana was turned over to the resistance. John Hartwick, along with a few other men would try to lead the newly designated "Rebel Army". He didn't like that term.

He knew it was going to cause problems. But the media, having already designated them "Rebels" and "Right-Wingers" would not stop.

He thought about his friend Matt Davis. Matt was black. If he found out John was leading a "rebel" army he knew he would lose him as a friend.

He also knew that if people thought they were a group of racists or white separatists, few would want to join. But there was nothing he could do about. He had to stay with the group and try to drive out the protesters.

Then he could get back to work and get back his life.

CHAPTER 5

FEBRUARY: A NATION ON THE BRINK

President Johnson met almost every day with Victor Van Driessen. This morning they were watching John Hartwick's interview and drinking coffee.

"What do you think of that guy?" Johnson asked.

"Who, Hartwick?" Van Driessen answered.

"Yeah. It looks like he is the leader out there in Indy. What do you think?"

"Hartwick is dangerous."

"Why's that?"

"Because he's right. There's a huge group of Americans that believe they've been ignored and abused for too long. Now the economy is in a deep recession and they see the writing on the wall." Van Driessen said.

"What do you mean? We're having hearings all this week to increase unemployment benefits."

"We've done that before. It's just a patch. It's not going to fix things, and they know it. If we come out of this recession in a few months, what changed for them? They go back to work for a few more years. The ones who lost their houses, their businesses, maybe they rebuild maybe not.

My guess is, just like the last time this happened, a few more will be kicked down a peg on the economic ladder. How many more can we let get kicked down?"

"So tell me, Vic, is this it? Is this the start of the civil war you were worried about?"

"Yes. Yes, it is. Look at it this way. There has been violence and death on both sides. And it's not getting better. Cooler heads haven't prevailed have they?"

"So do you think it gets worse?" Johnson asked.

"It's getting warmer. It will get worse. Mr. President, do we have any intel from NSA or the FBI?"

"Not yet, but we will next week."

The week passed, and not much had changed. The violence in Indianapolis had slowed, but in other areas, it was growing worse. St. Louis and Cincinnati were the worst.

In St. Louis it was becoming clear that the resistance was gaining strength. In Cincinnati, the battles were neighborhood to neighborhood and beginning to spill out into suburban areas. But neither side could gain an advantage.

The bigger cities of Chicago, Detroit and Cleveland were falling fast. But no one was winning. The riots in these cities were constant. In all three economic activity had stopped almost entirely.

Van Driessen and the President met again the following week in the White House Situation Room.

They were joined by members of Congress and the directors of Homeland Security, NSA, FBI, and the CIA. A senior analyst was tasked with filling them in on the current state of affairs.

"We can't get close to Ohlbinger. He keeps a loyal group around him and no one else. But what leaks out is disorganized right now. He is waiting, but we don't know what he's waiting for.

He flies every day. Either San Fran, LA, Seattle or Denver. He is planning something. But even he doesn't seem to know what it is yet. Or at least he is keeping it quiet enough that we can't hear it.

In the other cities there just isn't an organized movement from the right. The protestors are a bit more together and trying to hold them. Or if possible to take the cities. But right now it's just chaos. Fighting and resting. In the slow days, they are just resupplying. Both sides are doing it."

"You say you've got guys in Hartwick's group in Indianapolis. What's happening there?" Van Driessen asked.

"We don't know. They don't use cell phones much. And when they do it's just to arrange a meeting place. They meet in small groups and talk. If our guys aren't in the group, we don't hear anything. When something leaks out, it's usually just strategic information.

Thy move people around to give others a break. The let a truck or two with food into suburbs, and they slowly pinch in on the cities.

It doesn't look like they have any bigger plans other than taking the city back. But again, we can't tell. The group itself isn't what the media is reporting. Tanner Ritchie is not there. We think he is back in Missouri. They really do appear to just want the protesters out and to get back to normal. There is little coordination among any of the right wing, or rebel groups in other cities."

"What about inside the city. Any word there?" President Johnson asked.

"It's even harder to tell. The rebels cut off the internet into the city and knocked down a bunch of the cell towers. We do know from flyovers that someone is also taking out the power. Just transformers on telephone poles and one or two substations. But it's getting darker every night."

The Illinois Senator broke the ice on the topic everyone was thinking about, but afraid to say out loud.

"What can you tell us about Chicago? The word I keep getting is that even the mayor can't get into the city anymore. She and the governor both are asking me to get the National Guard involved. Mr. President, don't you think it's time?"

Before President Johnson could answer a congresswoman from Detroit spoke up as well.

"We're having the same issue. The protesters are being pushed aside by the people rioting. I can't get to my own house, Mr. President. I don't think we need to send the Guard to every city. But in the big cities, it's not the protesters causing the problems. Its outsiders and right-wing attackers. We need to do something."

"I agree, Mr. President. And I think we need to consider sending the military as well."

The room fell instantly silent. Victor Van Driessen scanned the faces. He could not read the president's reaction. Everyone else, Democrat and Republican was wide-eyed. Some frowned, some were smiling. Van Driessen guessed that most wanted the military involved.

The president looked to the assistant director of Homeland Security, who was giving the presentation.

"That's of course, a political decision Mr. President. But there is no government leadership in Indianapolis, Cincinnati, or many of the other cities either.

Some work is getting done. Somehow, people are working. But it's spotty. This is getting worse everywhere."

The president nodded and looked at Van Driessen. He knew Victor would speak his mind.

"That's a terrible idea." Van Driessen said.

"That's because you're from Virginia and it's peaceful. Our cities in Michigan and Illinois are being ripped apart." Someone protested.

More voices joined the protest.

"Mr. President, we're not suggesting you send in the Marines. Just the National Guard, and maybe some support from the Army. We need to get this under control quickly."

One after another, those who wanted the military to help peppered the president. After a few minutes Hank Hoxworth, the Vice-President, raised his hands to quiet them. "May I speak Mr. President?"

President Johnson nodded his head.

"We have to very careful here. The reason things are so far out of control is that the police can no longer manage the crowds. But I think some of you are missing an important part of this.

When the police go to block a street and try to control a riot, or stop a protest from getting out of control, they aren't going there to fight. They are going as a show of force. They are there to present the illusion of law and order.

If there are ten thousand protesters, and a city sends five hundred police officers, it only works if the people protesting have respect, or fear of getting arrested. That's it.

Once the people lose respect for the authority of the police, the illusion falls apart. Now the only way for the police to control the group is to start fighting. But in most of these cases, the protesters aren't armed. So the police can use tear gas and rubber bullets to fight.

Things are different now. The protesters are armed and don't respect the police as a legitimate authority."

"But that's why we are asking for the National Guard and the Army to work together to stop this." The Illinois senator said.

"That would make things even worse." The Vice-President responded.

"First off, it's illegal to use the military in this way. We can send the National Guard, but not the Army. But even sending the National Guard is a risk. Congressman Van Driessen and I have been talking about this for a few weeks now. There is simply no good option.

If we send in the National Guard, it looks like we've taken a side. And we can' just send a thousand troops. We have to send several thousand. Maybe as much as ten thousand.

Things are bad now. And they are getting worse. But if we make the wrong decision we could have a full-blown civil war on our hands."

He turned to the president.

"Mr. President, this is your call and I'll stand behind you all the way. But I think Van Driessen is right. This will make things worse. We are in something here. Something new.

Is it the start of a civil war? I don't know. But if we send in military troops, there will be no doubt, this is a civil war. There are just too many people at odds this time."

The president took a deep breath. "I guess you're right. But all I know is I want this to stop. This nation needs to come together. We'll hold off on the Guard, and the Army is off the table. But I've got to find a solution. We have to do something drastic."

It went this way for the next two weeks. Every day, in at least one city, many deaths would be reported. There were so many people involved and so much movement, that no government agency could say for sure what would happen next.

The loss of jobs in the cities had pushed the unemployment rate up yet again. But because of the violence, no one could get into the cities to count. So no one was sure what it actually was.

The only clear thing was that the recession was turning into a depression. From tax revenues, the estimate was that the economy would shrink by more than fifteen percent. More than during the Great Depression.

Even that wasn't a certainty. Because so much work could be done from home, the economy didn't collapse entirely. And tax revenues were sitting in some areas just waiting to be transferred. The rural sections of the country remained mostly unaffected.

Farmers delivered corn, wheat, soybeans, beef, and chickens. In some areas, these were processed into food that could be delivered. In other places, near major cities, the food would rot or be stolen.

Amid the protests and violence, it was impossible for Congress to pass any new laws. The left was paralyzed. It was impossible to figure out how many people actually supported the resistance. Polls showed the numbers were close to twenty-five percent. A manageable number, but they knew it probably was higher.

Other prominent Democrats were sure that many were just afraid to admit that they supported the protesters.

This was also true of the Republicans. The Democrats didn't trust the government in power. But most of the Republicans didn't trust the government or the media.

Furthering the Republican's problem, they weren't sure what the counter-protesters, the "rebel army" or their supporters even wanted.

The only group that appeared to have any organization was Hartwick's rebel army. And they hadn't really made any demands. Just vague notions on trade and immigration.

On issues where the Democrats and Republicans were close, they could never get enough votes to pass anything. Not only was the presidential election extremely close, but the Democrats held the House by two seats and the Republicans held the Senate by just one.

A compromise was discussed, but even on trivial matters, they could never seem to agree. The only thing the sides could agree on was that they didn't want to make matters worse.

Both sides held out hope that the other would get the blame and the violent factions would come to their senses.

February ended in a stalemate across the nation. The people in the cities were still fighting each other, but nothing was resolved. Congress was trying, but again nothing could be resolved.

CHAPTER 6

MARCH: THE FIRST VICTORIES

John Hartwick was resting at home. He needed a break. The money was holding out. He had received a paycheck and was doing some work remotely.

He had also received a few anonymous gift cards and envelopes stuffed with anywhere from five dollars to five hundred. But he wouldn't keep it for himself. That had to go to the other guys.

Too many were in a worse position than John. And, as he told his wife Audrey, he didn't want to be a mercenary fighter.

Sitting next to him on the couch was Matt Davis. He'd met Davis when he first moved to Indianapolis and they had become friends. They not only worked together, but Davis also lived just three streets away.

Hartwick had been afraid his friend Matt would think he was some kind of secret racist after his television interviews. So he made his way to his house and explained his position and why they had come to be called Rebels.

To his surprise, Davis had agreed with him and wanted to join him. He had been afraid because he thought he would be the only black man in the entire rebel army. When Hartwick told him they were just trying to get the city back, and there were other black guys helping him, Davis had joined willingly.

Davis had been with him several times patrolling the exits and moving food into the suburbs closer to the city.

In the first couple of days, it had been tough going. Some of the group thought he was a plant. But that had quickly been dispelled as more minorities joined the fight.

Davis was a project manager. He had a sharp mind and was an exceptional organizer. As they talked, Matt would have his laptop open and was constantly adding to his spreadsheets. He knew how many men they had, how many needed rest, what their strengths were and how to reach them.

He also knew what was going on in other cities and had started a line of communication with many of them.

"Cincinnati is having trouble John." He said.

"What's going on there? I thought it was mostly quiet." Hartwick answered.

"Nope. The media is just trying to keep a lid on it. The city is shut down and the protesters are holding it. There are some rebels, not as big as our group, but they keep going in trying to push them out. But they aren't having any success."

"You know Matt, we have to stop calling ourselves the Rebels. You more than the rest should know that's not a good look for us."

"Why?" Matt laughed.

Hartwick just smiled. "Look man, if we call ourselves the Rebel army the media are just going to call us a bunch of racists and rednecks."

Davis just shook his head and smiled. "John, I'm as black as night. When I came out to my own family as a Republican they called me a racist. Me, a black man, by my own family. It doesn't matter what we call ourselves. They are going to call us racists. Just embrace it and let it go. It really doesn't matter. I look at it as something I can throw in their faces. But you know what would really piss them off?"

"What's that?"

"Call ourselves the New Rebel Army."

"I don't get it. Why does that make it worse?" Hartwick asked.

"Because now it's got Rebel in it. Which they hate. And the initials NRA, which they also hate.

Hartwick shrugged his shoulders. "Well if you're okay with it, I guess I am. How did it go last night?"

"I think we're almost there. We counted twenty thousand leaving the city. There were so many we weren't able to search them all.

But the fires are spreading, John. We may have to go in."

"How soon?" Hartwick asked?

"I think we can get everyone together in two days. I really think it's necessary.

The remaining few thousand in the city could hold out a long time. We've questioned some of those that are leaving and they say it's getting worse. The resistance fighters are keeping what food they find for themselves. We need to do it quickly."

"What's the weather for the next few days?"

"Why?" Davis asked.

"Because if it's cold and raining, we should move then. We're rested and warm. They're hungry. If it's raining and cold, or even if there was a little snow, it would help us."

Davis flipped through the weather app on his laptop. "Tomorrow it gets down to thirty-two degrees and the chance of rain is sixty percent. Better chance Thursday and still cold. But then it starts to warm up all the way to the low fifties."

"Let's go Thursday morning early. That gives us two days."

The 'New Rebel Army' marched in on Thursday morning before sunrise. Davis had guessed they had a total army of roughly 8,000 people.

They would come in from four directions. The Southwest and southeast would have each three thousand men. From the north and east, they would attack with only one thousand.

To Hartwick's great surprise no forward lookouts had been posted. They simply walked into the downtown center without any resistance.

The last of the resistance fighters were holed up in three hotels. They surrendered quickly. Davis moved them all to the first few floors of each hotel. Ten to a room with guards posted at every door.

It had all been surprisingly anti-climactic.

Hartwick found Jake Stahl in the crowd. Stahl was the big bearded man who had worked with him from the start. At first, Hartwick thought he was a crazy redneck but the man was a natural leader and always calm and open to debate about what steps to take next.

Stahl had put five hundred men in each of the three hotels. He arranged for another five hundred to stay in the city. Everyone else was told to go back to the exits and stand guard to wait for orders.

"What now?" Stahl asked.

Hartwick suggested they walk to the capitol building and governor's mansion. When those were found to be abandoned they tried to go to the local police stations. There was no one to be found.

They stood in silence at the center of Monument Circle. "Well, ain't this some shit?" Stahl said.

Hartwick just shook his head. "I thought we could just go tell them the city is safe again and to open for business. But where the hell is everyone?"

"Typical politicians. They just ran away." Stahl said.

Matt Davis looked up quickly towards North Meridian Street. "Look at that." He said.

An old black man was strolling down the street. He stopped and looked at the men standing in the grass around the soldiers and sailors monument.

"'Bout time you boys got here." He said.

"Old man, what the hell are you doing out walking around?" Davis asked him.

"Lookin' for something to eat. Them communists that took over stole all the food." The old man replied.

"Did you kill them all?" He added.

"No. We just locked them in the hotel rooms until the police come."

"Shit boy. Police done left when the politicians did. You boys might as well get it over with and kill 'em all now."

"Why's that?" Hartwick asked.

"Oh!" The old man chuckled.

I guess you ain't been up to the convention center yet. Well, walk on up there fellas. And then when you're done, you gonna want to go back to that hotel and kill every last one of them fuckers."

And then the old man just turned and walked away. Laughing hysterically.

All three men looked at each other. "What's he talking about?" Hartwick asked.

Stahl, Davis and Hartwick walked to the convention center just a few blocks away. They took a hundred men with them to be safe.

As they got closer they noticed a slight smell. They walked to the doors and saw a few people run away. The men with them drew their guns, but no shots were fired.

Much of the glass at the huge front entrance had been shattered. As they stepped inside the smell became overwhelming. They walked through the grand entrance into the exhibition areas. There were dead bodies everywhere. They were not neatly stacked. It looked as if they had been herded in and executed.

Some wore police uniforms or security guard uniforms. Most were in work clothes. It was clear that they had been either at a convention or rounded up from local offices.

There were men and women but no children. The men mostly dressed in casual business attire or suits. Women in dresses or business dress as well.

Some of Hartwick's men started to walk forward. They instinctively pulled their shirts up around their faces to soften the stench.

At the back of the room, they saw a lone man searching the pockets and purses of the dead. He was stuffing money and jewelry into a backpack. One of the armed men pulled his gun and shot him on sight.

"The old man was right. We should go back to the hotels and kill every one of those animals." No one was sure who said it, but all nodded in agreement. Then Jake Stahl spoke.

"We oughta round up every Democrat in this city. Every bum and every fucker on welfare and ship them out to California where they belong."

Matt Davis stared at him. "I suppose you want to run out all the blacks to eh?"

Stahl lowered his head and shook it. "I'm not sayin' that Matt. But yeah, most of them probably gotta go."

Hartwick just stood silently looking at the carnage. He was rubbing his forehead with his fingers and trying to hold himself together.

"What do you think boss?" Stahl asked.

Hartwick didn't want to answer. He didn't want to be the boss. He didn't want to be in charge of this anymore. He wanted to be as far from this as he could. But he knew he couldn't. It wouldn't be right.

"Jake, the bums and the black people didn't do this and you know it. They didn't do it any more than you, Matt, or that old man who told us about this."

"Well, we ain't doing nothing!" Stahl roared.

"Someone's got to pay for this!"

Hartwick nodded. "Alright Jake." He then turned to Matt. How can we find out who was behind all this? And I mean the whole thing. The leaders, the ones who started all of this craziness." He said to Matt Davis.

"Go to the board of elections. Find out the big Democrat donors. Then go to IU. That campus is full of leftist nuts. I'll go get a few hundred school buses, and we can drive them out. But it can't be about race Jake. That's not right." Davis answered.

And so the compromise was reached.

"What about the politicians?" Jake asked.

"Fuck them." Hartwick answered. We'll run the city for a while. Go back to the lot where our own men are waiting. Find out who wants to be an Indianapolis cop.

Then let's get each of the groups to elect one person as a leader. No more than twenty-five or so. We'll get the city back on its feet. I'll call that captain, Andrews, from a few weeks ago. If we can get their help, we can at least get this city cleaned up. I don't much care about anything else at this point."

Stahl nodded and then reached his hand out to Matt Davis. "Davis, you're one of the best men I've ever met. I'm sorry about what I said. I truly am."

Davis shook the big man's hand. "I know you are Jake. I'm just as disturbed as you are. You did notice that there were black men and women lying on that floor didn't you?"

Stahl shook his head. "I know Matt. I know."

Later in the day, Hartwick decided to invite the media into the city. He held a short press conference at the front of the convention center, and then led them inside. The cleanup was on-going. Hartwick insisted that they film what had happened.

A reporter asked Hartwick if the mayor and governor were working with them.

"No. They all quit. The entire Congress, the mayor, city council and even the police have all left. It looks like most of the offices at the Capital building have been cleaned out as well.

Jake Stahl has been appointed governor and we are selecting one hundred men who have fought to save this city, to be in the state House. We are also going to contact every elected sheriff in the state. They will also be invited to join the legislature."

"So does this mean Indiana is seceding?" Another reporter asked.

"No. Not at all. We just want to get back to work and get our lives back to normal. We need to have a government. In our states time of need, our elected government officials all left. They've been gone for weeks.

We need a government and this is what we are doing. We have a police force in place, again from fighting men, and all businesses can open up tomorrow. You will be safe."

The scene was aired live. It was still early in Portland and Colby Ohlbinger was watching. Indianapolis had been as much as a surprise to him as it had to anyone. He told himself that it had always been a lost cause. Indiana was deep red. They were never going to hold that city.

But this looked bad and he knew it. If he didn't do something quick the protests would fizzle. When the protests died out, he would have no army to pull from. He picked up the phone and called his contact, Donovan Jenks, at CNN.

Donovan answered, "Colby, are you watching this?"

"I am." He answered.

"This doesn't look good for your resistance movement does it?"

Now it was "his" resistance movement he thought. The media certainly did turn quickly.

"You know what this is don't you?" Colby asked.

"What do you mean?"

"I talked to the Indianapolis leaders just two days ago." He lied.

"They were in the convention center. There was nothing like this going on. You are being lied to. The rebels pulled these people out of their hiding places and massacred them to set us up. Surely you know they are capable of this. Did you really think we would do it? What would we have to gain?

I'm going to be in Sacramento tomorrow night giving a speech. You'll get the truth there. Are you going to be there?"

Jenks hesitated. "I'll try Colby, but are you sure about this. This is bad."

"Trust me Donovan. Just be there. It's going to be the biggest rally this nation has ever seen."

"I haven't heard anything about it." Jenks answered.

"You won't want to miss it." Ohlbinger answered.

When he hung up the phone Colby got to work. He had not planned on going to Sacramento. But now he knew he had to. He called every media contact he could find. He knew the media would want a story and would report on the big rally. It was so easy. By reporting on a big rally, the media could create a big rally.

CNN was the first to report on the situation in Indianapolis. They also reported their conversation with Ohlbinger. But to Colby's dismay, they didn't buy it. They said that he was the only source and they could not prove that the bodies had not been there two days prior.

But other journalists were more questioning of the Rebel's story. The false flag narrative burned through social media in a matter of minutes.

The news media duly reported that a massive rally supporting the resistance was scheduled for Sacramento. Colby was successful. He made calls to Scotch Anderson and requested a meeting after the rally. He didn't need more money, but it always came in handy.

What he actually wanted, was Anderson to get him a meeting with the governor and other political leaders. But he would have to set the stage first at the rally.

Los Angeles was burning. The immigrants, mostly Mexican were sure that the Republican plan to deport them was going to happen. But that hadn't spread to San Francisco or San Diego. Colby had to change that. Somehow he had to bring them into the fold of the resistance.

He booked his flight and started working on his speech. He would only be taking a few people with him this time. He would need Katana to once again spread her peculiar form of violence.

He had an inner circle, a small group from Portland and the few left from Madison. He wanted to keep them close. Another group of about a thousand people was being paid with the money from Anderson. Not much, but enough to keep them full time. He knew that tens of thousands of others were with him.

The capital city of Sacramento was oddly isolated from the rest of California. It was close to San Jose and San Francisco, but still surrounded by Republicans. It would be perfect.

His speech was at the back of the capitol building steps, facing the small state park. Colby never understood how whenever he showed up, the microphones and the stage had already been set. It seemed to happen everywhere. He would just announce an appearance and these things would appear. He always stuffed a megaphone in his bag but lately never needed it.

In Sacramento, he shook hands with a few local politicians, state representatives and congressional representatives.

He hadn't bothered to learn anyone's name.

The crowd was listening to a radical feminist speaking. As he walked to the podium he could hear the crowd start to yell his name. He stood near the back of the stage as the woman ranted on. Talking, smiling and playing the part of the movie star. He made it a point to ask someone the name of the person speaking and indicated he would be going on next. No one questioned his decision.

As he waited he scanned his surroundings. There were police and security everywhere. In Portland, he had walked right in. He knew it would be different here.

He asked another person what the size of the crowd was. The police had estimated one hundred thousand, but more were coming in by the minute. The governor was a no show. Someone approached the woman speaking and whispered briefly to her and walked away.

She stopped speaking and turned to look at Colby. He motioned for her to keep speaking, gave her a big smile and a thumbs up and started clapping. The crowd went wild and started yelling his name. He waved at them and then pointed back to the lady speaking.

The woman knew she couldn't go on. So she finally relented and Ohlbinger sheepishly made his way to the podium. He kept saying her name over and over as he walked so he wouldn't forget. When he reached the podium he looked back to watch her walk away.

"Wendy Reese everyone!" He shouted. The crowd applauded loudly, so he motioned for her to join him.

"My gosh, Wendy. I'm so glad I got here in time to hear you speak. Friends, without people like Wendy, where would we be? Can we get just one round of applause for this awesome woman?"

The crowd applauded again. Colby stepped back to give her another moment. She wasn't even supposed to speak. She was a local leader of a very small LGBT group who had been asked to fill time. She had no idea what she was supposed to do, but she suddenly felt very important. Ohlbinger expertly guided her away from the podium.

He stood for a second to let the crowd silence itself. He was getting good at this. He knew what to do. He also knew that the crowd would have seen the video from Indianapolis. The first step was to diffuse that situation.

"Thank you all for coming. Thank you for letting me be here to join your cause. Your cause for something so simple it seems ridiculous that we have to fight for it. Why should we have to fight for justice? But we do." A loud cheer forced him to pause.

Drop the voice and make them strain to hear.

"It's starting to become clear, isn't it? The right-wing fascists in this country will stoop to any low. We know that now. I know you've seen the awful scenes from Indianapolis." He let them think for a moment.

He had worried that the media wouldn't show. He need not have bothered. They were all there. After Indianapolis, they wanted to hear what he would say. Most were convinced that he wasn't behind it. The media were convinced that it had been done by the resistance in Indiana. They had seen with their own eyes the execution of five men. They believed those five men were guilty. They did not believe the two hundred and seven bodies in the convention center were guilty. Ohlbinger was about to make them question everything.

When he thought the moment was perfect, when he knew everyone could hear him, he dropped his verbal bomb.

"And now, even the media wants the country to believe that we did this?"

He shook his head and laughed out loud. "How fucking stupid do they think we are?!" He screamed.

"Of course the rebels did this. We aren't going to be fooled. The Rebels are even fooling some of our so-called friends who are Democrats. But let me tell you something. We are now finding out that those people weren't all killed at the same time. So they want you to believe that our resistance movement was running around Indianapolis killing people and dragging them all through town back to the convention center. And yet somehow, when there were thousands of us in there, no one said a word.

My friends, fellow patriots, real patriots! We know the truth already. If you have any doubt, let it leave your mind. Don't fall for this absolute crazy nonsense.

There is no way this wasn't done by the right. The Rebel army is re-living the glory days of racism in the south. They did this.

When someone among you suggests that maybe a few of our fellow travelers got out of hand, you will know that you are talking to an FBI agent or a rebel insurgent. Get away from them and get them away from you.

And let me ask you this California. Where is your governor? The great Democrat, Margaret Wenner. Where is she? Do you remember when she promised healthcare for all of California? Where is it? Do you think she cares?

My friends, even some of our Democrat politicians are falling to the myth. The myth that socialism is bad. The myth that maybe we need to send some immigrants home.

I want to thank Wendy Reese again for the great work she does for the LGBT community. But we have to come together now. Millions of our friends in Los Angeles are fighting for their lives. You need to come here and fight with us.

Many of our African American friends are fighting for justice. You need to come join us. We are one people. One people that want justice for all of us.

Do not trust these politicians. Do not trust the media. They are corporate owned. Trust only yourself and your own eyes. We must stand together or we will all lose.

The reason this is all happening is that they know. They know! They understand that we have victory in the palm of our hands. They know we are about to overturn this farce of an election. We have the victory, but it must be our victory. All of us together!"

The crowd was now moving. He could see it and feel it. It was just like Portland. He just needed to close the deal. He wanted them to trust no one but themselves.

They would, of course be led by Colby Ohlbinger. He scanned the crowd again. They looked mad. They looked ready to fight.

It was a huge crowd. He looked around again at all of the police. There were hundreds. But the police weren't in the crowd. They were on the edges. He had the advantage in numbers. Katana was primed and ready. Now was the time to take California.

He turned with his back to the crowd to look at the capitol building. He paused for a few seconds and turned back.

"That's a nice building. Do you know who that belongs to? Do you know who paid for that? You did! It is yours. The park you are standing in is yours. So why are all these police watching us? What are they protecting? Governor Wenner doesn't own that building. The politicians don't own that building. We do.

Why in the fuck do we keep letting the politicians send out their storm troopers to watch over us like we are some kind of criminals?

We are simply taking back what has been stolen from us. You see that hotel over there?" He pointed to his left at the hotel across the street. Why are the police guarding that? Would you like to know?

Because that hotel also belongs to you. You bought it. Every time some politician stays in that hotel who do you think pays for it? You do!

Why are you out here camping in cheap tents, when your money bought that hotel? That glorious beautiful luxury hotel is yours. Just a few buildings away look at that! Another hotel that belongs to you. There is no other way to look at it."

He looked out towards the police officers standing along the road in front of the hotel.

"You police officers. Why are you doing this? Why do you fight for these liars and thieves? Look around you. Look at this crowd of nearly a million people. Do you not work for us? Either help us, or get out of our way!"

With the scream, he jumped into the crowd and walked towards the police.

That was Katana's signal. She had already made her way to that side of the park. But the crowd was pushing fast towards the hotel. Barricades were around the perimeter.

The police stood on the edge of L Street just behind the barrier. The two sides were face to face and the crowd was pushing.

Ohlbinger was behind them, in the middle of the crowd and cheering them on. Katana was now at the front of the crowd. She had lowered the backpack to her feet. Until the police used tear gas she wasn't supposed to act. It wouldn't work. So she waited.

After a few minutes, when the crowd wouldn't push any harder, she shoved the people in front of her.

"Take it!" She screamed. And the crowd rushed the police. It only took a second. Tear gas was fired from guns and shot from handheld canisters. She flipped open the front of the backpack and stomped hard.

There were three, two liter soda bottles in the bag. One was filled with bleach. Another was filled with cleaning ammonia. In the third was another concoction she had mixed herself which was designed to make the gas even worse. Her foot stomp in the middle caused all three bottles to push off the caps placed at the end, and the chemicals mixed.

Instantly the police and the crowd were in a panic. Katana could feel the burning in her own lungs and rushed back as quickly as she could. The crowd was stampeding around her. She tried to remain calm as she reached into her pocket and pulled out the smoke bomb she had made.

The crowd was beginning to get away quickly. She had no choice. She had to finish it now. She pulled the Zippo lighter and lit the fuse. Someone looked down at her. She just smiled and put her finger to her lips. The fuse hit the device and smoke poured out. She could no longer even see the people in front of her.

She pulled the nine-millimeter gun from her other pocket and fired all ten shots towards where she thought the police were. The police fired back.

Colby knew as soon as the tear gas went off what was coming. He backed quickly towards the capitol steps. When the crowd was preoccupied with what was happening he slipped out towards his rental car and drove away.

In two hours he would be in the Financial District in San Francisco. He was scheduled to meet with Scotch Anderson, the governor of California, and a few other prominent politicians and power brokers.

Colby was greeted at the lobby of the huge office tower. A friendly woman ushered him to the top floor in a private elevator. The doors of the elevator opened to a small waiting area. She ushered him to the left through two huge wooden doors into a wide open lounge area. It looked like a living room. There were four huge sofas arranged so that they all faced each other. Scotch Anderson walked up to meet him.

"Colby! We're glad you're okay. What happened there? It looked like the crowd got out of control."

Colby had easily anticipated this. He looked around the small group and spotted the governor.

"It wasn't the crowd. It was her Gestapo! He pointed accusingly at the governor. We were going across the street to protest in front of the Hotel and they stopped us. Then they fired some kind of gas at us. I thought it was tear gas but my lungs started burning. I don't know what the hell they were doing. Then they started shooting at us. I jumped in my car and left."

"Bullshit." The governor stood up and started towards Colby.

He immediately knew she wasn't going to be a pushover like the ones in Portland had been. She pointed her finger directly at his chest.

"You did this. You riled those people up and charged the police. What the hell did you think they were going to do, you idiot?"

Colby was momentarily stunned. This was the first real resistance he had faced.

"Well, you wouldn't know seeing as you weren't there, would you?"

"I wasn't there because you wanted to meet me here you half-wit. I think I'm done with this meeting Mr. Anderson."

Anderson tried to calm them down.

"Okay. Well, just, hang on a second. Why don't we all sit down and take a deep breath. I'm sure Mr. Ohlbinger is frightened about what happened. We're all on the same side here.

Racheal can you get Mr. Ohlbinger a drink. Colby what's your poison?"

"I'll have a diet coke." He wanted his mind sharp.

"Governor, I'm sure you don't want to accuse Mr. Ohlbinger of starting that riot. And Colby, I'm sure you know the governor is in favor of social justice and some expanded programs, so let's get beyond this."

"I do accuse him of starting a riot. You saw him. He riled those people up and egged them on." She replied.

"Someone needs to rile them up governor. Look, we're tired of this. We're tired of the empty promises from politicians. We're tired of the lip service."

"You are full of it young man. You have no idea what you are doing. You spout slogans about free healthcare and higher minimum wages. But you have no idea how any of this works. I've worked my whole life for those things and we have made great progress. You think it happens overnight and you can pay for it all with monopoly money. Then when you don't get your own way, you cry like a petulant child and create chaos."

Colby was becoming frustrated and angry. He wanted to pounce hard. But he didn't know what to say. Anderson came to his rescue.

"Madam Governor, Colby is really passionate. He is working hard and with his help, we can overturn this election. I know you want that" he smiled as he said it.

The governor just shook her head. "We all want that but this violence isn't the way to get it done. Look at Indianapolis and what your rhetoric caused there."

"We, did, not, do that." Colby said sternly.

The governor laughed out loud.

"Young man. Don't ever think that we buy the bullshit you sell down on the street. We know better."

Colby stood up. His fists were clenched. He walked out of the circle of sofas and towards the window to look at the city below and the ocean in the distance. He was beginning to lose control when it mattered most.

"Look Colby. I'm behind you. You know that. But the violence is bad. It's real bad. If we can't do business, how do you think we can fund you? How can we help if you bankrupt us?" Anderson said.

As he talked, Colby listened and thought. He was standing away from them just staring at the ocean formulating his plan.

Colby Ohlbinger could have been a great doctor, engineer, or chemist. He was incredibly intelligent. But this is what he wanted.

This is where his mind worked best. He was close. He just needed to bring it together. As Scotch Anderson continued to talk he said something that sparked Colby's mind. And he knew he had them.

"Hell Colby, my own car was hit by a rock from some protester just yesterday. And it's mild here in the city compared to other places. I mean, some of my friends are already thinking about bugging out to New Zealand until this blows over. I've got a place over there myself and I have to admit, I've considered it. You're going to start a civil war if you don't tone this down a bit."

A broad smile came across Colby's face. He saw a lone small wooden chair sitting off to his right. He walked over to it and picked it up. He carried it lazily to the center of the sofas. He put it down and turned it around so its back was facing Anderson and the governor. He lowered himself to the chair and crossed his arms over the back of it resting his chin on his arms.

"You people don't understand a damn thing. Do you think this isn't already a civil war?"

Anderson and the governor both tried to interrupt and Colby just raised his right hand. "Stop it. Both of you. Scotch you need to know one thing. This is a civil war and if you leave, you can't come back. If we win the resistance will say you were a traitor. If the right wins they will say you are the enemy. So if you leave, don't think you can ever come back."

Then he turned his head to face the governor. "And you have the audacity to accuse me of violence? Governor, you are either very stupid or insane. "

She tried to protest. Colby lifted his head from the back of the chair and screamed at her.

"Stop it! For years you were the one dividing this country! You told us every Republican was a Nazi. You told us they were out to get us. You said that elections were stolen. For years you told us we were the victims of social injustice. You told us they were destroying the planet. You filled us with righteous indignation.

And now? Now that we have listened to you, and start to fight for you, what? You want us to quit? You say they aren't that bad and it takes time? You say we are crossing the line? You started this. You did this. Every bit of this is your doing!

You've lived your entire political life riling up people like me. Okay governor, it worked. Your soldiers are here now. And if you abandon us now, if you in any way shape or form get in our way, I will make sure I see you hung from the capitol steps.

And I'm not speaking metaphorically here. I mean I will see your old neck being stretched by rope."

The governor was for the first time in her life silenced. She knew he meant business. And she also knew in some small way, that Colby Ohlbinger was right. He turned to face Anderson again.

"So it got too much for you eh Scotch? It's not your company that you can control every little detail, is it?

You did this too, Scotch. I read some of your blog. You were smarter than all of them, weren't you? Well, you won too. I am your soldier and I am here fighting for what you said you wanted.

Now leave me alone and let me finish it. Or leave. Go to your bugout mansion in New Zealand. But like I said Scotch, don't think you can ever come back. And don't think that your money is going to follow you. All that money you gave me? It's gone Scotch. I bought rifles and ammunition with it. I've bought and stolen tens of thousands of guns."

He stood up and pointed to the window.

"They're out there now Scotch. The Governor's soldiers are out there fighting for what she told us we should be fighting for. And we aren't going to lose.

He turned around and looked at the rest of the silent and stunned faces. "You're all in this now. Every last one of you."

He pulled his phone out. Flipped on the camera and scanned it around the room. When he was done he hit send.

"Johnny, you get that?" Colby said into the phone.

No one was sure he was talking to anyone, but they were too afraid to question him. He hit the end button and put it back in his pocket.

"Now I have my insurance for the ones I don't know. I need more money. I need millions. I need a million in cash and I need millions more in bank accounts that I can access from anywhere. Make it happen"

He started to walk towards the door and stopped.

"One last thing. Don't any of you ever act like this wasn't you. Don't ever act like you didn't do this. If it hadn't been for you people, I wouldn't be doing this. People have been killed because of your politics. Don't ever fucking pretend that this is anyone's fault but yours. All you have done here today is expose yourselves. I believed you."

He took a short step towards them and they flinched in their seats.

"Do you know Steve Oxley?" He asked with tears in his eyes.

"I killed him. I did it because I thought he would threaten what you set me up to do. So, please. Either get the fuck out of my country or get behind me and do as I say. But don't ever act like you are innocent.

He looked at the governor. Her entire physical appearance had changed right before his eyes. Her shoulders were drawn in and she was sunk deeply into the back of the sofa.

He pointed his finger at her. "You! I want a press conference tonight. You are to blame the police for this and tell them you are calling for an investigation. And at the end of that speech, I better be a national hero and my supporters all better look like angels.

He then looked at Anderson again. I need the money tonight. I'm at the Hyatt."

As he walked out of the room, not a word was said. In the coming days more than a million immigrants would converge on Sacramento to join his army. He controlled the state of California.

CHAPTER 7

APRIL: CIVIL WAR

Tanner Ritchie was with his people.

The news of Ohlbinger in California, and Hartwick and his group taking Indianapolis back did not help matters. He had been organizing for two weeks all over Missouri and as much as the south as he could reach. His army was over five thousand and growing daily.

Hartwick pissed him off further by calling himself the New Rebel Army. The south would always be the rebels and he wanted to exploit it. But he would not associate himself with the northern fighters. They were just as soft and weak as the resistance socialists and communists.

He had several lieutenants he could trust. They had all agreed not to make the same mistakes they had made in Indianapolis. Every night, small groups would enter St. Louis and kill. They were snipers. They would kill and move on.

Because of the activity in Oregon, Indiana, California and so many other places St. Louis had been ignored by the media. This worked in Tanner's favor.

The riots in St. Louis had quieted down. And Ritchie took credit for this. The killings and harassment by his "White Army" would continue. This created fear and brought the protesters back out. But only during the day.

That peace dividend worked in Tanner's favor as men from the suburbs began to join his army.

Some who joined would quickly leave. Once they found out that Tanner and his White army really was an army dedicated to creating a white nation they left. But many remained.

He funded his army by robbing banks. They would hit them not with four or five men, but with five-hundred or more. Within weeks most of the banks around St. Louis were forced to close.

Across many other areas of the south, there were fellow warriors. White separatist's armies were active in Mississippi, Georgia, Arkansas, Alabama, and even Florida.

But none were nearly as big as St. Louis. While the left wing resistance was gathering in Portland, the separatists were gathering in St. Louis.

Hartwick's new rebel army was, in the eyes of the media, the resistance, and the left, just another wing of the white separatist army of Ritchie.

This mischaracterization would prove to be disastrous.

In Indianapolis, the story of blacks, Hispanics and other minorities was much the same as it had been in California and other places.

The criminals and those who lived in poverty stayed out of it. The same was true of white people in the small industrial towns across the Midwest.

The white people who were poor and dying of Heroin and Fentanyl stayed away. Both groups, poor blacks and whites knew this wasn't about them. They had been forgotten for decades and saw no reason to fight.

In St. Louis it was different. Black people from the suburbs joined the fight. They were educated and had money. They had good jobs and wanted them protected.

They knew what Ritchie's army do to them, if he were to win. So they fought back.

The cultural gap between inner-city blacks and those in the suburbs was just as big as that between whites and inner-city blacks. Yet, they worked together.

Marvis Jackson was, as much as possible, the leader of the black resistance. He was an accountant and lived in an affluent suburb north of the city.

But he had been born in raised in some of the toughest neighborhoods in the city. He knew his way around, and he knew the despair.

His experience as an accountant helped more than anything else. He had organizational skills and was a spreadsheet master. The numbers he looked at every day led him to believe they would win. But it wasn't coming fast enough.

Jackson figured correctly that at any given time Ritchie's army had about five thousand people. He knew they would come and go. His own army numbered in the hundreds of thousands. But it was difficult to get them all on the same page at the same time.

Last night he had finally convinced a few organized forces of several hundred each, to work in concert. He had assigned some men to spy on Tanner's army. He had even had success convincing a few white people to infiltrate the White Army groups. He knew that in the evening they would be sending out five groups of twenty to kill black people in and around the city. He knew where they were going and when. And he and his army waited.

The next morning Tanner felt the force of Marvis Jackson. All of the more than one hundred men he had sent out had been killed. They were ambushed before they ever made a single kill.

Making matters worse, the media had finally shown up. Not many, but a few reporters and their cameras were on the scene at one of the massacres. The entire affair would be used as propaganda from both sides.

Tanner was about to be interviewed for the first time since Indianapolis.

He made sure that two of his own men were behind the reporters filming. He positioned two pick-up trucks in front of the pile of twenty-one bodies.

He would only talk to the reporters if they filmed the bodies being loaded into the trucks.

As he spoke, behind him four men were working. Two would walk up to a body and lift it by the feet and arms. The faces of the dead could be seen. These men looked like average white men. The sympathy would be worth the cost in Tanner's mind.

One of the bodies was that of a young blonde man. He had been shot once in the chest and a small circle of dark blood could be seen clearly against his camouflaged coat. His eyes were open. Tanner saw the cameras of all three news teams pan away from him towards the face.

He pulled the cigarette from his mouth and blew a puff of smoke to the side. Tanner was dressed in a tight-fitting army coat. The American flag had been pulled from the sleeve and replaced with a conspicuous rebel flag patch.

"That young man right there," He said. "was a brave kid. I think he was seventeen, but he told me he was eighteen. His name was Johnny Willis. The kid was always smiling. And let me tell you something else."

He took another drag of his cigarette and looked intently into the camera.

"That kid didn't hate black people. No, he just loved his family and his country and he was tired of what was happening to it. He wanted the American his daddy grew up in. Where white people weren't afraid to go outside at night. Where he could get a good job and raise a family.

That's all he wanted. He was fighting for a better America. He knew where the problems were. And he gave his life, so people, yes, white people, could live free and unafraid. You think he is some stupid redneck. You think he is just some racist. But let me ask you this..."

As he said it he used the hand with the cigarette in it to point to the camera.

"Wasn't this kid Johnny here fighting for what you want?"

Tanner flipped the cigarette off to the side and went to help the men load Johnny's body into the back of the truck.

The report the news played that night didn't include any of the footage or of Tanner Ritchie interview. The story was that the rebel army of White Supremacists in St. Louis had tried to attack a peaceful black community and been defeated.

They also said that St. Louis was largely peaceful but that Tanner and his army had been trying to get into the city and do the same thing they had done in Indianapolis. Thankfully they had been unsuccessful and only three people over the past week had been injured.

This was also untrue. Tanner's army had murdered closer to three-hundred black people, Hispanics, and 'suspect white people', in and around the edges of St. Louis.

Tanner was prepared for this. He was certain the news would never run the footage. So he pulled together videos from the men he had planted to film behind him. That was the video that was posted on the internet. Despite a valiant attempt to censor it, Tanner's interview had been seen by more than four million people the first night alone.

The next day, the ranks of his army would double to ten thousand. The following day he had more than twenty thousand.

In the first week of April, just a few days after the interview, the media was acknowledging that the nation was in the early stages of a civil war.

In Atlanta Georgia, Amber Weigel was putting her two kids to bed. A single mother, Amber had managed to finally get a two bedroom apartment on the edge of the city. It was a safe neighborhood and the schools were good. Her oldest was in the second grade and the little one was in Kindergarten.

The protests and the rioters had made it impossible for her to go to work for three days. If she didn't get back to work in the next couple of days she would need to get a job at one of the fast food places in the suburbs or further out.

She had just told her girls she loved them and went to flip off the light when an explosion rattled her windows.

The girls jumped out of the bed and ran to Amber. She tried to hold it together. This was the closest one yet. She hugged the girls and let them sleep with her.

In the morning, she would try to call her father. She had to get out. She would load the car and as much as they could carry and leave Atlanta far behind. There was no other option.

She had to move back to the country and live once again with her parents. Someday this would end. She knew it in her heart. Someday she would be able to get her life together and raise her daughters on her own. But not now.

In Memphis Tennessee Jalan and Kiara Green were putting their kids to bed as well. Jalan was sitting in the living room watching the news from St. Louis. He had also seen the Ritchie video. Memphis had exploded over the last few days.

In the comfortable suburbs, he felt safety and insulation. But he also felt connected to the city. He had grown up in the suburbs. For two years he had been the only black kid in his class. Back in high school, it had been a little better. There were four or five black guys and about as many girls.

He knew what was happening in St. Louis was also happening in Memphis. A pang of guilt struck him. Kiara, his beautiful wife of fifteen years sat on the couch next to him.

"Jalan, can't you turn on something else? I don't want to see this."

He stared at her for a moment not knowing what to say. These were the things they did not talk about. The things they did not acknowledge.

They were successful blacks, living in what too often seemed like a white world.

"Baby, this is real. This stuff is getting bad." He said. "That's why we live here Jalan. That's why we raised our babies out here. I know this is wrong, but you didn't grow up like I did. You grew up out here in the safety. You can't appreciate it the way I can."

He nodded and looked back at the television.

"Please baby, this stuff scares me." She said.

He smiled at her and changed the channel. Then two shots rang out, and the front window was shattered.

He pulled her on to the floor and dove on top of her. It was silent for a moment, and he heard another few shots further away, and then the sound of tires squealing.

He crawled towards the front door. "Go check on the kids!" He yelled.

He raised his head just above the sill to peak outside. All was quiet. He could see tail lights leaving at the end of the street in a hurry.

He cautiously stood up at the corner of the window and looked around. Porch lights were flickering on one by one.

He ran back and made sure the kids were okay when he heard the doorbell ring. They all froze.

"It's okay. I'm going to go see who it is."

On the way to the front door, he stopped in the kitchen. From the knife holder on the granite island he pulled a butcher knife out and held it to his side. He crept to the door as the bell rang again.

"Jamal, It's Bill Whitacre from next door. Are you guys okay?"

Jamal opened the door slowly. "Yeah Bill, we're okay. What happened?"

"I don't know. I just heard the shots and the glass breaking." When I saw the car speed away I came outside and saw that your house had been hit. My God. Are you sure everyone is okay?"

"Yeah. We're fine. Just a little shaken up. Come on in."

Bill walked in and looked at the glass shattered across the living room. "Oh my, look at that." He said as he pointed to the ceiling. There was a hole in the ceiling going up towards the kid's rooms. Jamal instinctively ran upstairs and checked the kids again.

There was another hole in the floor and then another in the wall just a few feet above his youngest sons bed.

Jamal sat on the bed and put his head in his hands. He was trying not to cry.

Whitacre walked over to Jamal's son Zion and stroked the boys head softly. He was only seven years old and seemed to be in shock more than afraid.

The doorbell rang again causing them all to jump. Bill stood up. "You stay here, I'll get it."

Through the night several more neighbors came. All were white, but that was to be expected. On his street, Jamal's was the only black family. An hour later, as five men were sitting in the living room talking about what they could do the doorbell rang again. It was James Willis. The father of the only other black family in the neighborhood.

"I see they got you too." He said.

"You mean they shot at your house as well?" Jamal asked.

"Yep. And as far as I can tell, you and I are the only houses that got hit. So we know what this was. We need to get the hell out of here."

The other white men in the room were silent. "Where the hell we supposed to go?" Kiara asked. "

We'll be safer here than in the city. We are black Jamal. It's not like we can run off to the country."

One of the men, a former Marine captain spoke up. "You'll be safer here. She's right. And we're going to help. All of us need to get together in the morning and form a neighborhood watch. We'll take turns. Every night we patrol the neighborhood with guns. We're all in this and we'll fight together." He said.

"Who are we fighting for?" The other black man asked.

"Ourselves." Jamal answered.

It was like this in cities all over the country. Black and white fighting against each other, but sometimes with each other.

White and white fighting against each other, and sometimes with each other. Left and right fighting against each other.

Only the people in the rural areas escaped the violence. For some, weeks would pass with life going on as normal as possible. And then for a few days, all hell would break loose.

For others, near big cities, the violence was nearly constant. When it was quiet for a few days and people would relax, it would flare up again and even worse.

Still, in other areas, it was as if nothing was happening at all. In small cities and towns in the Midwest and south, cattle and crops would be raised and processed. Trucks would come and try to make deliveries. Even in big cities some neighborhoods remained peaceful.

Boston, New York, and Philadelphia had protests, but they were largely peaceful.

A civil war had started, but no one could say who was winning.

In Indianapolis it looked like the right, or center-right would hold. In California, and most of the west coast the left were firmly in control.

On the East coast, it was the establishment. The tense but workable coalition of Democrats and Republicans, each afraid to cross certain lines, that held things together. In the south, outside the cities, life went on as always.

Young men would occasionally leave and join Tanner Ritchie, or some less radical side in the cities of the Midwest. In Texas, there were occasionally problems in Houston and Austin. But peace was holding and the protests that turned violent were quickly put down.

Back in Indiana, John Hartwick was home. In the three days since they had taken Indianapolis things were returning to normal.

But today would be his last normal day for a very long time. Two visitors were to change the course of his life forever.

The first was Scotch Anderson. He nervously rang Hardwick's doorbell. At least ten armed men guarded the house. He had brought only a bodyguard with him. He'd explained to the men guarding Hardwick's home that he was just here to help.

When Hartwick opened the door he thought Anderson looked vaguely familiar.

"Hello Mr. Hartwick. My name is Scotch Anderson. I'm the owner of one of the largest social media companies in the world. I've made some mistakes, and I'm here to try and correct them. May we talk for a moment?"

"What's in the bags?" Hartwick asked.

"We already checked them." One of the guards answered. It's just money. He's clean. He knows if he tries anything he won't get out alive. We checked them both."

Anderson motioned for his bodyguard to stay outside as he walked into John's house.

"How can I help you Mr. Anderson?"

"I've made a huge mistake Mr. Hartwick. And I'm not alone in that mistake. A group of fellow business owners has been helping Colby Ohlbinger out in California. He now has the entire state in a vise. We've given him money and he has bought guns, bulletproof vests and God knows what else. We thought we could control him. We were wrong. He's gathered the leftists, the immigrants and every other group you can imagine. He has a very loyal core of thousands who will fight to the death. It's gotten out of control.

We started this war. The billionaires and the millionaires who wanted cheap labor. The politicians who divide you for power. The Hollywood people who were so easily duped into believing in our cause. We did this. We never thought it would come to this, but it has."

"Well, I don't see how I can help with this. Our battle was here in Indianapolis. We won and we just want our lives back to normal." Hartwick responded.

"There is nothing you can do for me." Anderson said. "I have dug this hole and I can never get out of it. But you can help save the rest of the nation. I've learned my lesson. I know I can't convince you of anything. All I can suggest is that you don't join up with that Tanner Ritchie in St. Louis.

I hope you don't, but I know I have no credibility left. From the few interviews I was able to see, I think you are a good man. A better man than I am.

There are several million dollars in these bags. I am giving them to you to try to even the playing field and to give you a fighting chance. I can't control what you do with it.

There are no strings. I'm just hoping. Hoping that I can salvage a little bit of myself, and that you can save this country.

There are more bags in the trunk of that car. You can have your men bring them in. Buy guns Mr. Hartwick. You'll need them. When I leave here I'm going back to California. I have to. I am stuck trying to fix the mess I helped create. I will never tell anyone I gave you this money. If you tell anyone, I will be killed. It is your right to do that. I'm not even asking that you don't. I just want everything in my life to be honest. So you know it will lead to me being killed.

You should have no sympathy for me and you should probably shoot me right now."

Hartwick laughed and put his hands up, palms out towards Anderson. "Look, I'm not going to tell anyone and I don't want to shoot anyone."

"You say that today because you are fresh off of a victory. Trust me Mr. Hartwick, in the coming weeks and months, you will wish you had shot me. I have spent the last ten years trying to become the richest man in the world. I wanted to change the world. That was to be my legacy.

Now I will be considered one of the people who destroyed the greatest country that ever existed if you don't win."

Anderson got up and walked towards the door. He stopped and turned to Hartwick. "I wish you luck. I really do. But you will never see me again. I have to go back and pay for my mistakes."

He started to turn again but Hartwick stopped him.

"Anderson!" Anderson lowered his head. "Yes Mr. Hartwick?" He asked softly.

"Do you have kids?" Hartwick asked.

Anderson was confused and felt a threat. "Yes, but I have moved my children and my wife and extended family out of the country."

"Those kids are your legacy. Those kids and your character. You can't buy a legacy. No one has ever been able to do that. Think about the great men of history. Washington, Jefferson, Churchill, James Madison. Those men are remembered for their character.

You know those second-generation Hollywood kids that are always in trouble? You know the rich kids, who are always acting like fools and in trouble? What's the first thing you think of when you think of those idiots?"

Anderson thought for a moment then smiled. "They must have had some bad parents." He said.

Hartwick just smiled. "Thank you Mr. Hartwick."

The second visitor that would change his life was Matt Davis.

"John I've been talking to some friends in Cincinnati. They are struggling. That city should have been an easy hold for us. But they are being driven out. Dayton is already lost and no one is even trying in Columbus. They want your help."

Hartwick left his wife and kids again. It was getting harder to do. But Scotch Anderson's talk had convinced him that this was a battle he had to join. He took two-thousand men with him to Cincinnati.

They did the same thing they had done in Indianapolis. They surrounded the city and waited them out. It only took two weeks this time.

Then he moved north, taking Dayton and Columbus the same way. Each time they put local men and women who had fought with them in charge.

Cleveland and Detroit would be skipped. They weren't sure the sacrifice would be worth the victory. They moved east and south taking cities one by one.

Many times the victory would be on before they even arrived. The victors were always glad to see Hartwick. It was his plan, surround and contain, that was working everywhere.

There were deaths on both sides. Sometimes dozens would be killed. Hartwick's New Rebel Army would get anxious and try to attack too soon.

Other times Tanner Ritchie's supporters would engage the battle and slow them down. Hartwick tried to avoid fighting on two fronts and was usually successful.

If they weren't, they backed out and regrouped. Patience was the key to victory.

But the results didn't change and the strategy didn't change.

In Kansas City, Charlotte North Carolina, Pittsburgh, Des Moines and other cities all over the Midwest and even in the south. The same tactic worked.

They would surround the city at a beltway or stop the traffic from the interstates. At night, they would infiltrate and cut the power lines. On the edges they would cut off the cell phone service by cutting the communications lines to the towers or knock down the towers themselves.

Once the food and power were cut off they simply waited. If a city tried to counter-attack they would simply pull back or move around.

After the attempted counter-attack they would infiltrate again.

Often just two or three men would slip inside the city in the middle of the night and create chaos. Overpasses in the city would be blown up or knocked down. Transformers and sub-stations would be riddled with bullets.

After a few weeks, some of the smaller cities would simply surrender when Hartwick's men showed up.

But Tanner Ritchie and the White army held in St. Louis. The battles were constant and spreading. The White army was growing stronger.

Marvis Jackson's black opposition army was also growing. Something would have to be done but no one could come up with a plan.

Hartwick would never join with Ritchie.

He also didn't want to lose to the resistance. A socialist paradise was a pipe dream. The division that had been fostered couldn't be solved by free health care or a twenty dollar minimum wage.

The seeds of hatred that had been sown weren't going to be fixed by more government spending. He was becoming more ideological by the day.

There was no escape. This was a war. He had chosen a side and he would do the best he could.

CHAPTER 8

MAY: THE PEACE PLAN

T he negotiations in Washington D.C. had started in early April. Both sides felt that progress was being made. But the events in St. Louis, California and other areas had brought a fresh sense of urgency.

Both sides were committed to ending the violence. The words "civil war" were not spoken. But all knew it was here and had to be stopped quickly.

The President had decided to forego the tradition of meeting in the White House for high-level meetings. He went instead to the Capitol building.

He began with a summary of the issues.

"These are the areas we must resolve today. I think on most of these we are very close. So let's finish this up today if possible and then start the media push.

Number 1: Immigration. The Democrats agree to close the border with Mexico. The legal H1b and other immigration programs will be stopped entirely for two years. Then they will resume but only at 5% of current levels.

Number 2: Existing immigrants. Anyone who has come in the last ten years is to be deported.

Number 3: Health care. We will expand Medicare and open it to anyone who wants. But, taxpayers will have to pay 6% of their salary directly to the program. Those who wish can maintain private health insurance and avoid the tax.

Number 4: Abortions will be outlawed after the first trimester."

A Republican member spoke up. "I thought that was going to be up to the states. The states with heartbeat bills could keep that."

A Democrat responded:

"No, that's not what we agreed to. We think the first trimester restriction is draconian enough. All states will have to follow."

"Can we just drop this issue for now?" The President asked?

There was no opposition. So he continued. "These are the top issues that polls show have a high likelihood of buy-in from most Americans. This is our best bet for stopping the violence."

"What about the election Mr. President" It was the Speaker of the House. He had not wanted to bring it up. And it had been agreed that he wouldn't. But he was getting incredible pressure from the California contingent. There were eruptions throughout the room from both sides.

The top ranking Democrat continued despite the protests.

"We have to address this. It is the top issue in our polls. The election was never faithfully counted. Wisconsin's vote should have been a recount. It didn't happen."

The bickering continued back and forth and no progress was made on the issue. The Democrats wanted the president to force Hank Hoxworth to resign. Doug Swindell, the Democrat candidate would become Vice-President. Some thought that Johnson should then resign and Swindell could appoint him to be Vice President.

The president leaned back in his chair. He watched the bickering continue. They were so close. There was no guarantee it would work, but they were close to trying something. He watched and listened.

He realized the problem. They had bought their own propaganda. They were not just divided, they were insulated from the real world. He was not.

As President, you had to see as many people as possible. A Congressmen or senator had to do it once. Then they were almost always reelected. In safe districts, it was a one-time campaign and a spot for life.

He looked at Hank Hoxworth. Handsome Hank. The brilliant playboy. A man with a lust for life. He would never force him to resign. He was one of the few with any sense at all.

He thought of his supporters. Immigration and tariffs had been his keys to victory.

The left had mocked him. They thought he wanted to turn back time. They thought he wanted to stop technology and return to the fifties. In some ways they were right. Technology for the sake of technology was dangerous. It wasn't progressing society, it was regressive in many ways and for most people.

He thought to his years as a child. His father was an engineer. There were seven kids in his family. So he had to make his own way. He had been successful. Entered politics as a maverick businessman.

For the first three and a half years, things had gotten better. Then it had all fallen apart. He knew he was divisive. But he also knew he was simply playing the game that they had created.

He cleared his throat loudly and the room quieted. There was still at least some small piece of respect left for the office. Everyone in the room looked at him.

He slowly closed his trademark black folder in front of him and stood up.

"You are close. You are very close. If you would just come together on a few issues, this could come to a stop. It might not, but it could. If you come to an agreement and then every day talk to the people.

Put the cameras in every meeting. Declare a national emergency and force every television station and every radio station to broadcast it live. You would be forced to work together."

And then he stood up slowly. He walked around his chair and pushed it into the table.

"But I cannot force you to do this. And I am perceived as too divisive. You Democrats and those in the media have done this. You have painted me as a racist, bigot and an idiot. I cannot lead.

You are correct. It was a close election and, Wisconsin was never recounted. But neither was North Carolina. But my friends, that is all water under the bridge.

We can't fix it now. The Democrats are correct. Too many people will not accept me as their president. So effective immediately, I shall resign. Vice-President Hoxworth is the president of The United States. I will go back to the White House, pack my things and leave."

He walked out of the room.

There was silence. Hoxworth stood and took the President's spot at the head of the table. After a long few minutes, the Speaker of the House spoke. "Mr. President." He said with a smile.

"I think that now we can stop this war. We must come together and thank President Johnson for this great sacrifice for the nation.

I will also suggest tomorrow that the first memorial for a living president be erected in Washington D.C. for President Johnson. He has shown us all the way."

There was some polite applause but Hoxworth just stared ahead.

"I would suggest we suspend this meeting until Douglas Swindell can be contacted and brought in. We will vote immediately to name him Vice-President. If you chose not to resign, of course I still think we may have problems, but we have a good starting point. I hope that you will consider the president's sacrifice and follow suit.

If you do I will be open to re-appointing you, or any other Republican as Vice-President. And then this war will end."

After finishing Speaker Polawski bowed graciously towards Hoxworth and took his seat.

President Johnson had thought that things would unfold the way they had, and had requested the Chief Justice of The Supreme Court to be at the Capitol building. As soon as the speaker sat he walked into the room. A bible in his right hand.

"Vice-President Hoxworth, I am here to administer the oath of office of President of The United States."

Hoxworth stood and took the oath. When it was completed another polite round of applause. The Speaker stood again.

"I have texted Mr. Swindell. He is in Washington and will arrive shortly." The Democrats this time burst into a raucous round of applause. The Republicans sat stunned staring at Hoxworth.

Victor Van Driessen started to leave. He would resign as well. The farce was more than he could handle. But Hoxworth stopped him.

"Sit down for one second Vic." He said.

Van Driessen remained standing and stared at the new president. "I beg you Mr. Van Driessen, just one more minute. Then if you decide to leave I will not protest."

Van Driessen grudgingly sat and continued to stare at Hoxworth.

The new President stood.

"You should call Mr. Swindell back, Mr. Speaker. He will not be the Vice-President. I intend to nominate Congressman Victor Van-Driessen."

The room erupted. Half in protest half in applause. Hoxworth raised his hand to silence them. It didn't work so he yelled.

"Stop it! We are still in a civil war. Do you wish to make it worse? Did you really think that driving out President Johnson would fix all of our problems? How?

Outside of California and New England, he won in a landslide. He played by the rules, he won the Electoral College. This was a farce. He resigned to give you one last chance. I do not intend to piss it away. How could you have ever thought for one minute this would work?"

Speaker Polawski stood to face Hoxworth.

"We could have used the media. They were willing to go along with the entire story. They were going to push the compromise and were willing to hail President Johnson as the greatest American since Washington. This would have worked."

"Bullshit." Hoxworth responded. "This was never going to work. The media has no credibility and hasn't for years."

"That's not true! Polawski screamed. The crazy right doesn't trust them, but they don't trust anyone. Most people trust them."

"Again, bullshit." Hoxworth said. "The left doesn't trust them either. They listen when their narrative is supported. But it's confirmation bias. They have no credibility."

The speaker sat back down and crossed his arms in front of him.

"So what do we do? What's your great plan now?"

"I am the president. You are congress. What is your plan? I will execute it."

"So you don't intend to help?" Polawski asked.

"Do you have a plan? Outside what President Johnson laid out, which you had agreed on, and then changed your mind, do you have a plan?"

"Mr. Hox.., Mr. Vice-Pres..." Polawski stopped to clear his head. "Mr. President, we have to do what our constituent's elected us to do. They will not settle for this. So everything else is off the table. The California contin..."

Before he could finish Hoxworth cut him off. "The California contingent and probably half of the rest of the Democratic Party is controlled by Ohlbinger and his California crew, so cut it with that. They elected you to lead. Do you intend to lead or not?" Hoxworth said.

"We have offered what we could. We can do no more. You were supposed to step down when President Johnson did. You lied to us."

"When did I ever say I would do that? When did President Johnson ever say he would?"

"I will do what I can do to keep the nation together. Mr. Van Driessen, do you agree to be the Vice-President of the United States?"

Van Driessen was stunned by the turn of events. "I do."

He answered.

That night the media led with the story and the drama surrounding the resignation of the President.

Although some networks led with the Democrat charge that it had been a double-cross most did not. The media knew they had a credibility problem and they were determined to fix it.

The massive corporations that owned most of the media were tired of the profit losses. They wanted it stopped. Word had come down to hold opinions and just report the news. Most followed, some did not.

Hoxworth closed the border to Mexico. It was largely symbolic as most immigrants outside of California were trying to get out of the United States. But his loyal supporters applauded the gesture.

The Democrats who weren't attached to Ohlbinger or the California leaders formed their own resistance on the East Coast. They would fight to hold the center.

Some Republicans joined in the effort. They had petitioned all heads of the armed forces for help. But there was unanimous agreement among the military. They would not be involved in a civil war. Their job was to protect the nation from foreign threats. This was not a foreign threat.

The plan from the left was to form an impenetrable line of defense protecting the East Coast. It was well organized and well-funded.

Throughout the nation the supporters of President Bill Johnson were outraged. More joined Hartwick's forces and more joined Tanner Ritchie.

The outrage extended to the left as well. Johnson and the Republicans had screwed them again. Nothing had changed.

The Second Civil War was now officially engaged. There could be no turning back.

CHAPTER 9

THE LONG HOT SUMMER.

The Midwest was generally calm except for four primary areas. Chicago, Detroit, Cleveland and St. Louis. All but St. Louis were besieged by rioting. St. Louis was in a clear state of war.

In St. Louis the White Army fought the Black Army. The resistance tried to hold the city, and were supported by the local government. In Jefferson City, the resistance fought with those loyal to John Hartwick's new rebel army. Small skirmishes were frequent but seldom grew in size.

These skirmishes however made it impossible for the state government to help in St. Louis. This same scenario was playing out in many states in the Midwest.

There was no challenge from the right in either Chicago, Detroit, or Cleveland.

In Chicago, things were starting to quiet down. The resistance pressured the politicians on some issues but they were aligned and working together.

In Detroit, no one was sure what was happening. Cleveland was much the same but hundreds of thousands had moved out.

In cities all over the south and Midwest, millions of people were on the move. Buses loaded with people, either willingly or forcefully were removed to California.

In St. Louis, Tanner Ritchie's army had grown to nearly fifty-thousand. Many were not White Supremacists or separatists. They just wanted the fighting to stop. There was no other group to join so they joined his rebel army.

The New Rebel Army of John Hartwick was well organized and governing. They had no desire to enter the fray of St. Louis.

The hope was that over the next few months, one side or the other would gain the upper hand and a decision could be made to attack or not. But over the last few weeks, since the resignation of President Johnson, things were spinning out of control

The White Separatist Army had sealed much of St. Louis. But they still suffered casualties by the dozen or so every day. They controlled the suburbs, exurbs and even some of the rural areas.

They were also sending men out to disrupt other cities. Atlanta and Nashville experienced frequent battles because the center-right, aligned with Hartwick, couldn't battle to hold the cities and fight off the Rebels.

Tanner Ritchie and his group had too much control over St. Louis and that gave him a base of operations. There had been some grumblings among the Hartwick's army to join up with the Southern Rebel army. As time passed Hartwick knew this would be tougher to contain.

He also knew if he did this, he would be abandoning his friend Matt Davis, going against his own beliefs, and lose the support of most of the American middle class.

So today Hartwick's 'New Rebel Army' was to hold a large meeting. The biggest they had ever had. The meeting was taking place in Springfield Illinois. Close enough to St. Louis to be a rally point, but far enough away to be hidden from Tanner's army.

Five hundred leaders from around the Midwest and south had gathered. Hartwick chaired the meeting but insisted any decision must be decided by vote.

There were many who wanted to join with Ritchie's Southern Rebels. Hartwick wanted a vote that was closer to eighty percent in favor of fighting against Ritchie, but the number was just under half at the start.

Many men protested that they were not racist, but joining Ritchie was the quickest way to win.

In a strange twist, it was Matt Davis, the black man, who convinced them to fight and not join. He was speaking on the numbers.

"We have over three-hundred thousand soldiers ready to fight. Several hundred thousand more can be made available within weeks.

The SRA of Tanner Ritchie has at least one-hundred thousand. However, they only have about fifty-thousand around St. Louis. At least, that's our best guess. The rest are scattered from Nashville and Atlanta, to Houston and Kansas City. I know most of you aren't virulent racists. Well I hope not," He laughed.

Luckily the crowd joined in on the laughter. "And I think you just want to join Tanner's SRA to avoid a longer war and deal with him later." There was loud applause at this notion.

"The problem I'm seeing here, other than for myself!" He tried to ease the tension again. There were a number of black men in the crowd, but they were a tiny minority. But again there was laughter so he grew calmer.

"The problem is that we are going to lose a lot of support from the middle class and you'll lose support from those on the East Coast.

If we want to keep the country together, we need those groups.

Guys, if we think back to the eighties, we were doing great. Blacks and whites were starting to get along pretty well. Something happened to divide us again, but I think it's more shared frustration than anything else.

If we can put America first, bring back the jobs, and grow the economy, we can return to a better day. Remember we've had the media coming at all of us for years."

He paused for a second and threw out a question he thought might work.

"There are five-hundred people here and probably only ten or twenty black guys. I know there are more back home supporting us, but let me ask you black guys a question. How many of you have been called racist by your own friends, or even families for supporting President Johnson? If so, stand up."

Every black man in the room stood.

"Now keep standing. I have one more question for everyone. You white guys. How many of you have been called racist for supporting the President, or being opposed to immigration? Or any other so called 'right-wing' issue like guns, abortion or just being a Christian. Now you guys stand up."

Every person in the room was now standing together.

"So can't we fight together?" Davis asked. A loud cheer went up and the vote wasn't even necessary.

The plan was set. They would gather as many soldiers as they could.

Davis also told them that there were desertions from the United States Army, Marines and Air Force. Not many, but a few thousand. They would now have some real military expertise.

They would converge on St. Louis from the north. Fifty miles outside of St. Louis they would split into divisions.

To start they would leave Springfield and the largest group would travel down Interstate 55.

Others would move west and travel down 67. The last groups would go all the way west and follow I-70 into the 270 loop that surrounded half the city.

Once they had control of the entrances to the city, they would find and defeat the SRA.

Once they had defeated the SRA they would withdraw to the beltways and close off the city. Then they would slowly pinch in, just as they had done everywhere else.

Davis had identified Marvis Jackson as the leader of the black army. They would work to contact him and then determine if he would continue to fight the New Rebel Army by joining with the left, or be open to a peaceful return to normalcy. No plans could be made beyond that point.

It took two weeks to get everything organized. As the armies moved towards St. Louis, Hartwick was becoming worried. They were over confident.

This was going to be something they hadn't faced yet. Hartwick and Davis both joined the group that would attack from the west. The first wave would come from the east.

The rally point was at a big intersection well outside the city. The army of ten groups of two thousand split up on 64 twenty miles from the East loop, which was 255. Another twenty thousand would be split into a group of ten thousand to the west and ten thousand in reserve. They would send forty-thousand men on the first wave.

When they had defeated the southern rebels they would bring in another one-hundred thousand to take the city.

Hartwick and Davis were with a group at the front. They stopped and used binoculars to scan the interchange exit ramps.

Their troops kept off of the main highway just on the side. They could see no traffic on the loop, and very few cars moved along I-64.

Two thousand men in their group were hiding in an industrial park just on the north side of 64. Across the highway was farm land. No one was moving anywhere.

Behind what has called "Group EA" was "Group EB". These were the East groups. Off to the south Group C and D would be getting in to position. These men would be arriving in about thirty minutes. They would converge on the farm area with more than ten thousand when all was set and take the interchange.

"What do you see?" Hartwick ask one of the men with binoculars.

"Not much. There are twenty or thirty armed men on the overpass."

Hartwick looked behind him for the sergeant. He was one of the military deserters who had joined the group. He had combat experience.

"Hey Sarge! Can they see us from here? Or are we okay to move in to position in the farm land?"

The sergeant grabbed the binoculars and scanned. He could see nothing other than the men on the overpass. But they were still more than half a mile away.

"Let's circle back to 157 and then use the trees as cover along the south side. Then we can surprise those thirty or so men up there and take the overpass."

Hartwick nodded. They used cellphones to call the other groups to have them maintain positions. Even if there were twice the number of men on the overpass Hartwick and the sergeant agreed they would have no trouble taking them.

As they moved south there were no problems. After just a few minutes they saw the tree line and turned towards the cover and the overpass. They were trying to stay low and move slow.

The sergeant grabbed the young kid with the binoculars. He raised his hand to get the line to stop so he could make sure nothing new had happened.

"What do you see kid?" He growled.

"Still just the same thirty... Oh holy shit!"

The first shot rang out dropping the young soldier. The sergeant was hit next and fell dead instantly. From the trees was a barrage of gunfire and rebel yells.

Hartwick grabbed Matt Davis. "Get to the back, get to the back!"

They fell back as quickly as they could. After running a hundred yards he noticed everyone else was retreating. Some were yelling to hold a line and return fire. A few stopped and fired blindly in front of them towards the trees.

This stopped the advance, but the gunfire continued. A small creek offered cover and hundreds of men jumped in to take positions. But most just kept running.

Hartwick and Davis were on the southern edge crouched down and peering cautiously over the bank.

"Call group B to the south and tell them to return fire from the flank."

Davis nodded and fumbled for his cell phone. The gunfire slowed to a few shots every minute. They were pinned in at the front, and too afraid to run to the back.

Hartwick and others were able to rally enough of their soldiers to fire back in between the enemy fire and stop them from advancing. But some shots were now coming from the fields to the North West.

Davis was screaming into his phone so Group B could hear. As soon as he hung up he told Hartwick they were coming. He tried to call the group behind them. The second part of group A but his phone buzzed first.

"What!" He screamed as he answered.

He couldn't understand what the person at the other end of the call was screaming. "Calm down! I can't hear you."

The person started to talk again but more gunfire drowned out his voice. Davis waited a moment for the gunfire to stop and then told the caller to try again. He could hear gunfire on the other side.

"This is Jones from Group N, we're getting slaughtered up here. We tried to call the west group but they are engaged as well. We're pulling out! Get up here and help us or meet us back in Illinois!"

The call ended.

For twenty minutes gunfire was exchanged sporadically. Then it began to pick up and Hartwick could see the enemy soldiers were slowly advancing.

"We better get the hell out of here!"

Someone from his right yelled back at him. "We can't. As soon as we stand up and get out of this creek bed they'll mow us down!"

"How many do we have left?" Hartwick yelled.

"Don't know. Along this little section of creek it looks like about two-hundred, maybe three hundred tops."

"How many do they have?"

"Can't tell that either. But there are more coming off the overpass. Hundreds more probably."

"So it's fight or die?" John yelled.

"Looks that way sir!"

"You a soldier?" Hartwick asked.

"You mean right now? Yeah!"

"No, I mean were you in the army or marines or something?"

"Yes sir. But I've been out about ten years. Saw combat back in Afghanistan."

"Get over here!"

The man crawled over and settled between Hartwick and Davis. "What's your name soldier?"

"Troy Evans sir. I never rose to sergeant in the army, but I did see a lot of fighting."

"Well, what the hell should we do Evans?"

"Best bet is to hold our position and try to contact Group B behind us. Get them to crawl up here, and from the creek bed we can form a line. We should be able to wear them out."

Evans looked over Hartwick's shoulder to the man crouching to the left of him.

"Dobbsy, is that you?"

"Hey Troy." The man answered.

"Sorry sir, just makes you feel good during battle to see a familiar face."

"Davis, can you reach Group B behind us?"

"No luck. I keep getting calls from the north and West groups. West is pulled back about five miles. They think they lost about one hundred killed. But the group is holding a line, they're just too far back to help.

The North group is in real bad shape. They are heading back to Springfield. That was our biggest group and they say they have already lost thousands of men."

"You mean thousands ran away?" Hartwick asked.

"No John, thousands killed or wounded.

"So, at best we're down to what, twenty-thousand men?"

"No John. At best I figure we have five-thousand men. I'm calling back to Springfield to get them to come here and get us the hell out."

"What would you do Evans?"

"Sir if we can't reach them by phone we need to send a couple of runners back to get them."

"All right then. Evans, you've been given a battle field promotion. You're Colonel Evans now. Let's get ourselves out of this jam." Hartwick said.

Troy Evans smiled and saluted Hartwick. Evans was the kind of soldier who was in trouble during his time in the military. He chased girls and drank too much. He was also the guy that never got in to as much trouble as he deserved.

He was on the short side of six feet tall, a little too skinny, and had longer hair than most military men. He smiled constantly and it always looked like he had more teeth than could possibly fit in his mouth.

When he left the army he went to college for a year but didn't like it. So he got a job selling cars. Then he got married and quickly had a young daughter. When the economy tanked he was one of the first to lose his job. When things started to get bad in Indianapolis he knew he had to do something.

So he had joined the gang north of the city at the same time as Hartwick. And now, he was somehow a colonel. He realized it didn't mean much, but maybe he could help get these guys out of here.

"Dobbsy! Get your shit together and run like hell back to the east. Keep going until you find Group B. Tell them to crawl once they get within five-hundred yards. Slow and steady." Evans said.

The young kid 'Dobbsy' started to stand but Evans stopped him. "Hang on! Someone needs to go with you."

"I'll go." A man to Evan's right said.

"All right. Let us get some covering fire for you."

Evans rallied the men quickly. He was going to count down on his right hand from five to a fist. When he made is fist all were to start firing on the enemy until they needed to reload. He told ten men closer to him not to fire at all.

When the covering fire stopped they were to wait. If they sensed it was calm they could stand down. If the enemy detected the lag, return fire quickly so they thought we weren't all out.

"When you two see my fist, run like hell but stay low."

He raised his hand, fingers spread wide apart and counted down. When his fist clenched Dobbsy and the other man scrambled out the back of the creek and started running. The barrage of gunfire was deafening and Hartwick knew instantly something was wrong. Men started falling left and right.

"Stay down! Stay down!" Evans yelled.

About half of the men had stood up to start firing. The rest correctly peaked over the bank to fire. Of the men who stood many were instantly killed.

Hearing Evans yell to get down, most of the rest of the men stopped firing.

Evans looked behind him. Jimmy Dobbsy, the young kid he had met on the way down, just eighteen years old, was shot in the back and fell dead. The other man kept running.

"Ten, return fire but stay down!"

The ten men held in reserve started firing. When their ammo was spent it was quiet.

"Fuck! Fuck! I'm hit!" Hartwick was screaming.

"Easy man easy."

Evans leaned over to him and wiped the left side of Hartwick's face. His glasses were cracked and Evans knew it was a shot gun blast.

"It's just a shotgun blast. It broke the skin but you're okay."

Hartwick calmed himself and wiped his face. He could feel the bbs under his skin. There were only two, but the one in his forehead was bleeding enough that it ran into his eyes.

All around him men were moaning. Hartwick wiped his face with his sleeve. Evans yelled instinctively for a medic. A lone man with a backpack scrambled towards him.

"You're it?" Evans asked?

"Yeah. We started off with twenty but I think the rest left or were killed."

"Shit. Fix up Hartwick and then get to the other men."

For several minutes the soldiers helped to patch up the wounded. The dead were covered with coats and blankets.

Hartwick and Davis sat with their backs to the enemy along the bank of the creek.

"How did I ever get myself into this mess?" Hartwick asked.

Davis shrugged his shoulders.

"Is this worth it?"

Davis shook his head and put his finger to his lips. He leaned towards Hartwick. "Don't say that out loud man. Keep your cool."

Hartwick nodded that he understood. He regained his composure and took his hat off. He searched around for a stick and stuck the hat on the end of the stick. He slowly raised the hat. Four quick shots rang out and the hat was gone.

"Them southern boys are some good snipers eh?" Evans said.

Hartwick just nodded.

"Alright, listen up!" Evans yelled. "Everybody reload. When we see Group B coming we're going to need covering fire again. Keep low. Just peak over the bank and fire. You don't have to be accurate. We're just trying to stop them from firing on us for a minute. Last ten guys on the edges. You guys shoot more north and south to your direction. Ten guys in reserve, same thing as last time."

And then they waited. A shot or two would zip overhead every few minutes.

Someone yelled out. "They're coming. I can see them crawling this way."

"Okay, everybody get ready. Same thing. On my clenched fist start firing. But keep your damn heads down and your bodies low!"

Evans waited. The men were all staring at him intently. When the few random enemy shots started to pick up, he knew Group B had been spotted. He started the countdown but at four he stopped.

"Shoot slow. Don't empty your mags too quickly. Just a shot every second or two. That will give our guys more time."

And then he resumed the count.

At first, the men in Group B stopped. Then they realized it was covering fire and they all sprinted for the creek bed. Only two were hit.

When the initial barrage was complete Evans told the ten reserves to get ready. When the enemy returned fire, he clenched his fist.

The second barrage started and hundreds of men poured over the edge and into the creek bed.

Evans organized the men as quickly as he could. He found other men with combat experience and made them sergeants.

As he crawled back to Hartwick he noticed a man with two backpacks following him.

"What do you need soldier?" He asked.

"Can you find Hartwick? I've gotten something for him."

When they made it back to Hartwick the man unzipped the backpacks. He was an older guy. Mid-fifties with graying hair and a scruffy beard.

Most of the man had some form of camouflage. But this man had overalls and a baseball hat. Over his right shoulder was a rifle. Around the middle of his overalls at the waist he wore a belt. Tucked in the belt were two revolvers.

"You Hartwick?" He asked.

"Yes I am. What can I do for you?"

"I got a present for you. I'm a farmer up in Indiana. We use Ammonium Nitrate and diesel fuel to blow stumps out of the ground. So I made you some hand grenades."

The man opened his backpacks. In each one were five footballs. Then he emptied his pockets and there about twenty M80 firecrackers.

"These are just backups." He said. Sticking out of each of the ten footballs was a fuse. "I tested these back on the farm. The fuse gives you about four or five seconds to throw the football.n

Light it and let it go quick. They're a bit heavy, so you really gotta heave them. If you don't throw them far enough, the bad guys could throw 'em back. So throw 'em far." He smiled.

"It's ammonium nitrate?" Evans asked?

"Yeah, but I also packed some nails in there to give them some extra kill power." He smiled.

"We may get out of here yet." Evans said.

"John, Matt, let's round up the ten guys with the best arms and clear these bastards out."

Davis and Hartwick nodded and then Hartwick raised his hand.

"Wait a minute. We still have guys pinned down up north and maybe even out to the west. Why don't we through three of them and keep the rest? If three works, we can take the rest and try to help the other guys?"

Evans looked to the farmer who had built the bombs. "How powerful are these things farmer?"

The man inched his way towards the banks. "Show me where the bad guys are at." He said.

"Most are directly ahead. Some may be just thirty or forty yards away. From what I can tell the bulk of that middle group is about right there.

Off to the right and left there are two smaller groups. Mostly snipers. I think they are about fifty or sixty yards back. It's hard to tell."

"How wide are they spread?" The farmer asked.

"Just that tree line. I figure there must be a good thousand men bunched together right there. More came down later so I don't know how many are behind them. We can see them move back and forth though. At least a few thousand all together."

"Two of them footballs will clear out the front easy enough. But you'll need to make sure you throw them as far as you can. The snipers on the edge you should get as well. Those are gonna blow nails out for about fifty years around them easy, maybe a hundred."

Evans looked at Hartwick. "How about four. Two in the middle and one each on the edges."

The plan took another few minutes to come to fruition. Four of the best throwers would launch the football bombs. The rest of the men would be in firing position. When the smoke started to clear they were to start firing.

When the footballs were flying through the air Hartwick said a prayer. He knew if this didn't work there wasn't much chance of getting out alive.

The explosions caused a ringing in his hear louder than he could ever remember. Davis was yelling at him but he couldn't hear a single word. He turned and started firing. The enemy were in a frantic retreat.

John Hartwick had his first kill. He saw the man running away through the scope of his newly acquired rifle and pulled the trigger. The man fell instantly.

He scanned and fired again. A miss this time. The adrenaline was coursing through him and he could feel his heart pounding in his chest.

Another appeared in his scope. He fired. The man stumbled and grabbed the back of his leg. Hartwick kept him centered. The man rose and started running again. He aimed for the center of the back and fired. Another miss as at the last second the man had darted to the right.

He raised his head away from the rifle. The shotgun blast he had taken to the face had shattered the left lens of his glasses. He could see figures moving around and lowered his head to look through the scope. He fired one more shot and missed again.

"Cease fire! Cease fire!" Evans yelled.

After a few more seconds the guns fell silent. There was no return fire.

"Let's get the hell out of here." He said to Hartwick.

"We have them on the run, shouldn't we advance on them?"

"Hell no. We have less than a thousand men. They have at least a few thousand more. Maybe much more, who knows?

We need to swing around and head to the north. If we charge, they'll take up position on the other side of that freeway and start picking us off. We need to go sir. We need to go now."

"Let's get out of here boys." Hartwick screamed. He looked to the farmer.

"You stay with me or Evans. And thanks farmer."

They talked as they ran. After a few hundred yards they were able to walk. The cars were still five miles behind them. The newly appointed sergeants got the men who could, double timing the march. Many fell back. It was nearly two hours before they were back at the big parking lot, well outside of the range of fire. But they were still nervous.

Hasty plans were made to rally to the north and try to rescue the N groups. Davis had finally contacted a few of them on the walk back. They were holding out, but down to a few thousand men. The news from the west group was much worse. They had been surprised and flanked on both sides.

The injured had been carried off and fifty men were left behind to guard the hospital as they were treated. The dead were left lying in the creek bed and the fields.

Davis and Hartwick sat in the back of a truck. Davis was working his spreadsheets in furious fashion. After just a few minutes he slammed the laptop closed.

"I have no idea what's going on. We may have lost half our men John."

"What the hell happened?" Hartwick asked.

"You have spies in your group." Evans answered the question from the front seat of the truck. He was in the passenger seat.

"What?" Hartwick asked.

"It's the only explanation. Someone in your group is a spy. Probably several. How do you vet your soldiers? I know no one asked me anything."

"What do you mean?"

"You have to find out where these guys are from. If a man shows up alone, let him join, but keep him in the dark about everything.

You guys did a great job of dividing your forces the way you did. Multiple attacks on several fronts should have worked. But the enemy knew the plan. You need to keep information on a need to know basis."

"Shit." Hartwick said. "How come none of these military guys told us this?"

"That's another problem John. You have no real chain of command. The sergeants you did have, not the military just the ones you put in charge, they just look to you. You need a chain of command.

You be the general. I'll take one of these armies of four or five thousand. And I want my sergeants from this battle. Then find another colonel and put him in charge of another army."

Hartwick was just nodding. "What else?"

"Well, you need to get your guys some firing practice. Did you see how well those southern rebels could shoot? Your guys can't do that. It's a big problem."

"Yeah, our guys are mostly from the suburbs. We just haven't been in a fight like this yet. Everything else went smooth compared to this shit." Hartwick said.

"Well, it will get better. But the next time we try this, we need a few weeks to prepare."

The farmer with backpacks was driving. "Hey farmer, sorry, what's your name?" Evans asked.

"Jack Roark, pleased to meet you."

"How many of those footballs do we have left?

"Six"

"How quick can you make more? And how many?"

"About as many as you want. I have plenty of stuff to make them. I just ran out of footballs. They only take a few minutes. But I can't do it now."

"Yeah, I know Jack. John I think we bail these guys out in the north and head back home for a few weeks. We need to get a better plan together and we need more of Jack's magic footballs."

"We need a helluva lot more men to." Davis said.

"Naw. You had plenty of men. If they don't get a rush of new support here, you should have plenty."

They pulled into the parking lot of the next designated rally point. They were just five miles north of the fighting. Evans jumped out of the car and looked towards the end of the road they had turned from.

"Weren't those guys with us?" He asked.

There were trucks speeding away from them.

Hartwick nodded. "Well, yes they were. Shit. How many you figure we lost?"

"Looks like just seven or eight trucks. That's not bad at all. I figured you'd lose half."

As quickly as they could, the men gathered around Hartwick and Evans. They slowly marched towards the sound of fire. They could see their own men. As they got closer and the sound of gunfire grew louder, a few more bailed out and ran for home. Everyone understood.

Most of these men were not professional soldiers. Some had joined for the adventure of fighting. They left quickly. Others wanted to fight, but the terror of combat was too much for untrained men.

By the time they reached the line of trees that marked their defense point there were just seven hundred of the one thousand who had left the creek bed.

The woods were poor cover. But just a hundred and fifty yards beyond them was a long winding hill. The hill was not high, but it was much too far to throw the footballs.

Every few minutes they could see someone pop up from the hill and fire at them. Between the hill and the tree line was an open field. Several bodies were scattered around the middle.

"Those our guys?" Hartwick ask.

"Yep. We pulled out of these woods way to fast. They just mowed us down.

Had they waited two minutes longer they would have killed us all. But as soon as we stepped out they started firing. When we got back into the trees they were still chasing us. We had the other field behind us, so we knew we had to turn and fight. They backed off pretty quick and it's been a stalemate ever since."

"How many did you lose?"

"I don't know sir, I know it was more than a hundred. But at least four hundred more were shot and wounded. We lost a couple thousand more just getting those guys out to safety.

They gathered up what we could of the dead and they headed back to Springfield. Then about another half just deserted us. They kept running at the beginning and never came back. Can't say as I blame them. We were hoping you would bring more fighters. What's our plan to get out of here?"

"We have a surprise for you. At least I thought we did. We have football bombs. They are like hand grenades. But we can only throw them about thirty or forty yards."

"How are we going to get those footballs all the way over there?" Hartwick said to Evans.

"Battlefield engineering." Evans answered.

"What's that?" Hartwick asked.

"It means we need to figure something out."

There was some discussion to just leaving. The problem was that if they started to withdraw, the rebels would see it and could advance on them.

"If we had three old trucks, we could rig them up with the balls at the front. Then light the fuses, put a brick on the gas pedal and send them towards the hills."

They found three soldiers with old trucks who volunteered them. Anything to get them out of this mess. When Hartwick reached in to his pants pocket and pulled out two huge stacks of money to pay them for the trucks they were even happier.

Evans just stared at Hartwick as he peeled off the hundreds.

"I'll explain later." Hartwick said.

It took more than an hour to bring everything together. The farmer, Jack Roark, worked with some of the other guys to rig longer fuses together. Ropes were used to tie down the steering wheels so the trucks would drive straight.

The truck in the center and the truck to the right held course. But the truck to the left started to turn. Luckily it turned towards the center and was guided alongside the middle vehicle.

The bombs were attached to the front of the trucks. As soon as the fuses were lit the gas pedals were dropped and off they went.

The rebels, believing there were drivers in the trucks, opened fire. Fire was returned and all was chaos for several seconds.

As soon as the trucks hit the hill the first two bounced up and came crashing down. Just seconds later they both exploded.

The second truck kept going. It was ten long seconds before it finally exploded.

Hartwick and his soldiers hiding in the woods saw several bodies fly into the air.

Beyond the hill they could see men running everywhere. John, Matt, Troy Evans, and their worn out soldiers had their chance. There would be no more gunfire. They all turned and ran.

The rebels were sure that the United States Army was helping Hartwick's group. There was no other explanation for the bombs, as Tanner Ritchie had said.

But the southern farmers knew exactly what had happened.

Two days later, Hartwick gathered the remaining men in Springfield. Of the forty-thousand who had started there were less than 9000 left. Half had simply returned home. But eleven thousand men had been killed or wounded.

Hartwick drove to Indianapolis to pick up the bags of money left by Scotch Anderson. He gave fifty-thousand dollars to Troy Evans.

To the six sergeants he gave twenty-thousand. This was done quietly. To the other men who had fought, he offered to pay what they needed. If each asked for just one thousand dollars he knew he would run out soon.

Luckily most men refused the money. The ones who did ask for money ask for a few hundred dollars.

Three days later Troy Evans arranged for twenty men to go back to St. Louis for surveillance. They would try to blend in and get all of the information they could.

For the next two weeks, Hartwick and Evans built an army. A real army. Trucks were fitted with plate steel. Old car tires were used to make bullet proof vests and additional armor for the front of a dozen trucks. These would be the tanks.

Roark the farmer, worked with engineers and other technical people. They devised fuses that didn't need to be lit.

They also planned. Every day a group of men would drive towards St. Louis to meet with the spies. They discovered that they were building their own bombs and placing them in the middle of the road. They also noticed that they placed the bombs in the exact places they had fought in last time.

This was proof that they had kept the spies out of their own army. Only the people who needed to know, knew where they would attack next. And none of the previous battle areas were on the list.

On the day they were set to leave they had managed to arrange an army of only ten thousand. Others were helping, tens of thousands. But they did not want to fight.

Then a group of welders and machinists approached Evans and Hartwick.

"We've got something for you boys."

Behind them were two huge pickup trucks with the cabs and the beds covered in canvas. The men who had worked to build the trucks, together tore back the canvas and revealed something none of the men had ever seen or would have believed.

In the bed, over the top of the cab, were guns. Dozens of them all stacked together. They were on a swivel platform with a seat behind and a trigger device.

"You like it?" One of the welders asked.

Troy Evans was grinning from ear to ear. He ran up to the trucks and was counting. There were one hundred guns rigged together to two triggers. Fifty guns per trigger. The guns were each slightly offset from the ones below so that longer magazines could be fitted.

"Each mag holds one hundred rounds of ammo. In the tool box are one hundred more magazines. That means each truck can fire off ten thousand rounds of ammunition. It takes a while to reload, but we got cover for that as well."

Jack Roark spoke up.

"I made you five hundred bombs this time. Some boys had to steal the footballs. But we got them. The boys who built this helped with another couple of trucks. Hope you don't mind John, but we needed some of that money and Davis gave it to us to buy the trucks."

Hartwick and Evans were both in awe. The next two trucks had catapults on the back.

"These will launch them footballs about five hundred years. The fuses and catapults are all timed to work. You just press the button. Can you believe that? They made a fuse with a timer. We don't even have to light it."

Troy Evans looked at the trucks. "This is the kind of stuff those mountain Arabs made in Afghanistan." He said. "Battlefield engineering at its finest."

When the army was about to move out, Hartwick went to check with Evans so they could communicate during the fight.

"Hey Evans, I think you've done a great job. This feels like an army now."

"Thank you sir." Evans said, and then saluted Hartwick. He started to get in to one of the tank trucks and Hartwick stopped him.

"Troy!"

"Yeah?"

"It looks like everyone has a place to be and knows exactly what they are doing. Where do I go?"

"You don't sir. You stay back here."

Hartwick was flabbergasted. "What the hell Troy, I fought okay. I even killed a guy." He protested.

"Sir, this army needs one leader. You're it. If you get killed out there, the whole thing will fall apart. You're the general now. Your days of being on the front lines are over. You and Davis. You two and the data team stay here and coordinate for us. There should be at least ten thousand more men on the way here, right Davis?"

"Yes. We have commitments for a reserve force. Some are already arriving."

"Good. Keep in touch with all of us officers and sergeants and get them out to us quick if it goes as bad as it did last time."

Evans got back in the truck. The driver started to pull back but Evans stopped him.

In front of him were two men texting on their phones. One was a younger guy, early twenties, maybe younger. The other was late thirties, maybe forties. Evans watched. The younger man's eyes were darting around as he texted. Evans noticed he held his phone slightly away from the man and kept glancing at him. Troy jumped out of the truck.

"Hey you guys all set? You know who you're going with?"

"Yeah. Were supposed to wait for about ten minutes and then join the rear support group." The older guy said. A rifle was slung over his shoulder. The younger man just nodded.

"Where's your gun soldier?"

"The younger man smiled nervously. Sorry sir, it's back with my other gear. I'll go get it."

"Hang on. Do you two know each other? Are you brothers?"

"Yes sir. We're not brothers but we know each other." The young man said.

"This is Doug and my name is Jason Fitz."

The older guy, Doug, walked forward with his hand extended to shake Troy's hand.

"Doug Wilson, nice to meet you."

Evans shook his hand. "Who are you guys calling?"

"Calling my wife. Just want to tell her I love her before we had out." Wilson said.

Jason Fritz waved his phone quickly towards Evans and smiled. "Girlfriend sir."

"Okay." Evans said. "Sorry to bug you boys. It's just we've had some spies infiltrate from the Southern Rebels and we need to make sure everything's okay."

Doug pulled out his wallet from his back pocket.

"Those guys are the reason I'm fighting. I came up from outside St. Louis a few days ago. On the way up I stopped at a gas station and that's where Jason and I met." He took a few pictures out of his wallet and handed them to Evans.

"This is why I need to fight."

It was four pictures of small black kids. All were smiling. Evans knew instantly this was a proud grandfather.

"Oh so you guys just met."

"Well yes sir, Fritz replied. Evans noticed the kid was becoming visibly nervous.

He looked back to the truck and motioned the men to help him.

"Let me see that phone son."

"Why? You don't need to see my phone. I'm just texting my girlfriend."

Fritz started to run but Doug Wilson quickly grabbed him. Troy joined and they held him down and grabbed the phone.

Evans picked up the phone and started going through the texts.

The last text said, 'They are moving out now. Heading for the fields we talked about before. They are going to line up behind the hill. Should be there in two hours tops.'

Evans started typing into the phone.

'Slight delay. Something is wrong so they are regrouping. They won't be leaving for another two hours.'

"You know kid, in war spies are shot on sight." He turned to the men guarding Fritz. "Take him to Hartwick and tell him to question him and get every bit of info they can. Then throw him in prison until after the war."

Evans noticed the visible relief that washed over young Jason Fritz, and he knew he would cooperate.

The message he had sent to the rebels caused him to change his plans slightly. In five minutes he moved the battle trucks to the front and left in a hurry.

A mile outside of the designated battle area he knew the text he had sent for Fritz had worked. They slowed to a few miles per hour. There were rebel soldiers pouring over the hill into the rear areas. He saw spotters to his left and right. The rebels were trapped. They weren't expecting an attack for two more hours. The trucks raced forward that last mile and took position.

Bullets were flying in both directions but Ritchie's army had no time to take proper cover.

The two trucks with the multi-rifle machine gun contraption opened fire. In less than two minutes, twenty-thousand bullets had been fired into the enemy army and around the edges. Thousands of men fell instantly to their deaths.

When Evans saw the retreat was to the south, he moved the catapult tanks forward a few hundred yards and let the bombs fly.

These were much bigger than the football bombs. The explosions were enormous. The fuses didn't work perfectly, but even that had worked as an advantage.

When the bombs would fall silent for a few seconds enemy soldiers would stand and start running again. Then the explosion would rip through them.

Evans' soldiers began to feverishly reload the multi-guns. They would not be necessary.

Colonel Troy Evans, field commissioned officer, was certain he had his first victory.

He waited for five minutes and then ordered the troops to slowly move forward. As they approached the hill two lone footballs were seen flying through the air.

Evans turned and shouted at his men to pull back. But it was too late. The bombs, copied almost entirely from the ones the farmer had made two weeks ago exploded.

Dozens of soldiers from Hartwick's newly named 'New Freedom Army' lay wounded or dead. Right next to Troy a man had shrapnel rip through the right side of his body. He grabbed the man's left arm and started running back.

When he made it to cover behind a tree he bent to help the wounded soldier. He was alive but in shock.

Tyler bent down to him and moved the man's arm so he could see the wounds. He was bleeding badly out the right side of his chest.

"You're going to be okay." He said.

The man looked up at him. "I have four kids. I need to get out of here and get back home."

Troy pulled a bandage from his backpack and did his best to pack it around the wound. "We'll get you out. Medic!" He screamed.

But all of the medics were busy treating other men. Before they arrived the man had died.

When Evans had guided the rest of the men back to cover he sat on the ground and thought of his next move.

He had let his ego get the best of him. He wasn't a colonel with years of leadership experience. He was a corporal with about fourteen months of combat experience. But he was the head of this army. He needed to move cautiously.

Those men were killed because he had acted impulsively. He vowed to himself that it would not happen again.

He rallied his men. They would wait. For thirty minutes he sent spotters ahead in different areas to assess the situation. Only then would he move.

He took the hill with no resistance. But his spotters had noted that a few hundred yards ahead there were more rebels. Perhaps only a dozen or so.

Within two hours they were well inside the 255 loop. Evans split his army in to three groups. He would lead one division of two-thousand around the east. Another group of two-thousand would move south towards the city.

Six thousand would stay where they were and be called as reserves if needed. As Evans moved closer the resistance became softer. He called Hartwick and told him it was safe to come down. He then talked to Matt Davis.

The leader of the black army in St.Louis, Marvis Jackson was moving out of the city and finding little resistance. They would meet at the edge of East St. Louis in two hours.

When John Hartwick arrived Matt Davis was with him. The resistance had dwindled to nothing. They were less than two miles from the point where they were to meet Jackson's black army.

Evans left a trail of reserves behind him and continued towards the area with just two hundred men. More were just minutes away if needed. He walked casually and talked with Hartwick and Davis in the middle of the pack. Word had come through that there was intense fighting in Michigan and they wanted Hartwick to send help.

As they came close to the rally point they walked slowly through an industrial park. Conversations were muted but there was no sign of danger.

And then a first shot was heard. Seconds later enemy soldiers came from behind a group of buildings. Evans watched as his men reacted perfectly. They took cover and returned fire immediately.

It was clear they were outnumbered. But not by much. He called for another 500 men in the rear section to move forward slowly. He remembered to tell them to watch their flanks. He was getting better at the strategy.

Another football bomb was launched but it exploded harmlessly in front of them. Under cover of the explosion the enemy started to advance and Evans considered retreating to a safer position.

Then another barrage of gunfire came from behind the enemy.

He was about to order a full retreat until he realized the enemy had turned and were fighting the men behind them.

He needed to make a quick decision. He hesitated and Davis made it for him.

"Let's go! Attack!"

They moved quickly and shot at the retreating army. Those in the rear of the enemy formation turned to return fire but were quickly mowed down.

Evans turned back to his troops. "Hold here!"

Evans, Davis, Hartwick and ten other men inched cautiously forward, firing as they went. Over the din of fire he yelled at Hartwick. "You two are here again. Dammit! I should have made you stay behind the lines."

Hartwick smiled. "That's okay. This is fun."

They stopped at the edge of the park. On the far side was a fence. A hundred or so enemy were firing right across the fence. They couldn't climb over the fence and they couldn't retreat.

Evans called up the two hundred men right behind them. They began firing and bodies fell quickly.

"Cease fire! Cease fire!'

It was a voice coming from the other side of the fence.

Evans told his own troops to hold their fire. It was eerily silent.

"Okay, everyone move forward slowly. Get your guns ahead and keep alert."

All two-hundred of his men walked upright. There was no need to crawl and nowhere in the park to hide.

"Easy boys, easy." He yelled. He could see a dozen or so figures moving from the other side of the fence.

"I think that's Jackson's men." Matt Davis said.

As the two-hundred reached the fence a group of just ten black men met them. Both sides had guns leveled at each other. No one spoke for a long minute.

A man at the far end of the black army line dropped his gun and raised his hands. The others with him did the same.

Evans, Hartwick, Davis and the other men still were silent for a long few seconds and the black man who first dropped his gun, in the raspiest voice any of them had ever heard, tilted his entire body to the side and said.

"We ain't wanna fight no mo." And then he smiled broadly.

Matt Davis erupted in laughter, and then everyone else joined in. The guns were dropped and the men shook hands and hugged across the fence.

For the next several hours the Black Army of St. Louis and the New Freedom Army, formally the New Rebel Army, ate, drank beer and reveled in their victory. Jokes were made, often at each other's expense and stories told about the past.

Hartwick was sitting at a table with several older black men. One, a man who appeared to be about seventy-five-years-old was noticeably quiet.

"What do you think about all of this?" Hartwick asked the old man.

The man looked at John and smiled softly. "It's strange to me. I don't know who we are fighting or what we are fighting for." He answered.

Hartwick nodded, not really understanding what the man was trying to say. "Well, I think right now we're fighting for survival. If we can get through this, maybe we can all start to get along."

The old man shook his head. "No. I'm not too sure about that. I'm seventy-seven-years-old. When I was a teenager in the sixties, I knew my place. I was a black man in St. Louis. I had an education, but no college. I could get a job, but it had to be in a factory. And I was never going to get a good union job. Those went to the white boys.

By the time I was in my thirties things were getting better. Then, a few decades later we had a black president. What did all of that get us?"

"But what about your kids and grandkids?" Hartwick asked.

"Oh, they do pretty good. But, that's not the whole story is it?

When I was born, my daddy was fifty years old. That means he grew up in the 1920s. Back then, a black man had it even worse than I did. My daddy hated white people. And you might not want to hear this, but he had good reason to hate white people. My daddy grew up in a tiny shack alongside the Mississippi river. When it

flooded, they just had to rebuild it. They never had no insurance
and no savings account.

So rebuilding a little shack of a house could take months.
Sometimes even a year or two.

When the Great Depression came, their life got worse. And it
was already bad to begin with.

So I think he taught me to hate white people. I've gotten
better. I really have. I don't hate you. And, I know you boys came
down here and helped us. But you have to know this, there are
generations of mistrust. I hope we can fix this. But, a lot of black
people and a lot of white people are dying in this war every day.

And I'm not so sure any of you have a plan on what to do if
you win."

When Marvis Jackson arrived the conversation naturally
turned to what was next. The discussion was long and passionate,
but never disrespectful. Both sides were acutely aware that they had
lost friends in the battle just ended. And that created a bond that
would not be easily broken.

In the end it was agreed that St. Louis would be left to heal.
Tanner Ritchie's army was defeated, but they had done great
damage. Blacks by the thousands had been rounded up and put on
buses for California.

John Hartwick cringed at the news of this. For he realized
how he had dodged, just barely, a similar situation in Indianapolis.

The remaining resistance fighters in the city would have to
be dealt with one way or the other. Jackson promised not to fight

with them, but to try to work with them. St. Louis had seen enough bloodshed. Marvis Jackson wanted to peace.

By the time the media finally flocked to St. Louis Hartwick, Evans and their army were long gone. It was a story that would be told by Marvis Jackson.

CHAPTER 10

THE MICHIGAN WARS

J ust six months ago the Muslim population in Dearborn Michigan was about forty-thousand people.

When the news hit as Hartwick was returning from St. Louis that large battles had been raging in the city, the population of Muslims in Dearborn had grown to more than two-hundred thousand.

For years Muslims had prospered in the city. Businesses owned by Arab emigres had blossomed and life was peaceful.

When John Hartwick's strategy of isolation had been implemented in Columbus Ohio and victory declared, thousands of Somalian immigrants were forced out. The easiest and most natural solution was to move them to Dearborn.

Most were forced, but some went voluntarily. All were angry at the upset in their lives.

In a scene that was similar in many Midwest cities, it wasn't just Muslims. College professors who were determined to be left-wing were loaded into the same buses and shipped to Dearborn.

Then Toledo quickly fell and the process was repeated. Those considered left-wing agitators were forced out and ended up in Dearborn.

By the time June rolled around a bad situation was primed to explode.

In California and much of the east coast, there were celebrations after the fight in St. Louis. The left decided that the civil war was nearly over because the right wing armies were now fighting each other.

The media and many of the politicians on both sides agreed and started calling for a return to normalcy and a stop to the forced evacuations.

Before the new narrative had twenty-four hours to take hold, Sadiq Al-Samir attacked in Dearborn.

A loose coalition between the Muslims who were long-time citizens of Dearborn and the newly exiled undesirables who were white, black or Hispanic was formed.

But the resistance was poorly armed and badly disorganized. When the more moderate Muslims insisted that women and gays not be allowed to fight, the coalition fractured.

Within just a few days Al-Samir and his violent Islamic Army of the New American Caliphate were victorious. Non-Muslims were driven to the edge of the city and moderate Muslims were forced to submit. Every Muslim male sixteen or older was drafted into the new army.

In just weeks the city of Detroit was besieged. The Ambassador Bridge and the Detroit Windsor Tunnel were both destroyed.

Many of the men of Michigan quickly formed an army connected to Hartwick's New Freedom Army and moved to seal off Detroit at 275 and 696 to the North. They were pushed back beyond Ann Arbor and well north of Pontiac in days.

Information about the situation inside was nearly impossible to get.

Muslims from across the country streamed towards Detroit. Moderate Muslims inside Detroit left for Canada until the bridges and the tunnel were destroyed.

Desperately, some tried to pack up their cars and leave with what they could carry. They were however often detained by the New Freedom Army aligned with Hartwick and forced back in.

The NFA was so far outside the city however, that many could get in and out without much difficulty.

It was not uncommon for a caravan of Muslims leaving Detroit to pass another caravan heading in.

In Washington D.C. the consensus was that troops finally had to be used to quell the violence in Detroit. Van Driessen had warned Hoxworth against it. But Hoxworth relented and ordered the National Guard to fight.

Ten thousand men were called up to liberate Detroit and restore peace. Only four-thousand men showed.

The force would attack from the south along I-75 and storm into Detroit. They had no tanks and no armored cars. They did have big trucks that could hold troops and automatic weapons.

When they reached 275, south of the city they were to rest briefly and charge into the city.

But the north overpass had been destroyed. The National Guard troops tried to follow 275 West where they could quickly head north on 24.

When they were within a mile of the 24 exit they slowed. They were to head north to Flat Rock and assess the situation. If they needed to fight there, they would take Flat Rock and then rest before moving on to Detroit. Between 275 and flat rock was mostly farmland. If the exit was intact they were confident they could easily make the next step.

As they crept closer, they were relieved to see the exits not only intact but free of traffic.

As the lead trucks moved onto the ramp the entire group began to pick up speed. But as they were at the top of the overpass explosions rocked them.

Hidden roadside bombs caused the first ten trucks to plummet off the side of the overpass.

From the sides of the highway, hidden in the cornfields, bullets rained down on the guardsmen. A hasty retreat was made.

Hartwick left the next day for Michigan. He had set a meeting at Whitmore Lake about 15 miles from 275 and I-96. He took Evans and a few other military men with him.

The other leaders of the NFA were left to secure Atlanta, Nashville and other cities in the Midwest and South as needed.

The New Freedom Army was becoming more organized and more disciplined by the day. After the St. Louis victory it was also becoming much larger.

John Hartwick saw his role as organizing and strategizing with military leadership. And making decisions that would rightly be considered political.

As more men defected from The United States Military to join them, and more men from Texas and other areas of the south made their way towards Indianapolis, the leadership of the NFA became professional and structured.

His welders, machinists, and engineering team were creating more effective weapons as well. He and Troy Evans knew that it would all be needed to retake Detroit and the big cities on the East Coast if it came to that.

As they pulled into the meeting area near the lake Hartwick's phone buzzed. He looked down and recognized the area code immediately. It was 202. Washington D.C.

He looked at Evans. "This call is from D.C. Should I answer it?"

"Answer it 'General Hartwick, how can I help you'?" Evans insisted.

John shrugged his shoulders and did as Evans had said.

"General Hartwick. This is Admiral John Shock. I am the Chairman of The Joint Chiefs of The United States military. Do you have a moment to talk?"

Hartwick dropped his phone. "Shit."
He quickly picked it up and tried to regain his composure. "Sorry about that Admiral. I was uhh,... I was just getting out of the car and dropped my phone."

Evans was grabbing John by the shoulders and shaking him. He took the phone from him and told him to tell the Admiral to hold for one second. John did and then covered the mouthpiece again.

"John, I know you don't get this, but you are a general. You are his equal. You have to maintain your calm and act like you are a general. This is important John."

Hartwick shook his head that he understood and calmed himself.

"Sorry about that Admiral. As you can imagine we're a bit busy out here as you can probably imagine. What can I do for you?" He asked. He cursed himself as he realized from his sentence that Admiral Shock now knew he was nervous.

"General Hartwick first I want you to know, you can relax. You are a general. You have seen more combat than I have. I am not calling you General Hartwick for some political point's bullshit. I would never do that. It is out of respect General."

That put Hartwick at ease and at the same time made him wonder if the General had heard him.

"Thank you Admiral. I appreciate that. He took a deep breath and let out a sigh.

Look sir, this is all, well this is all new to me. I've learned a lot in the last few months. But I'm still learning and doing the best I can. I hope you'll bear with me. I am a little nervous. I'm talking to you and we feel like we're really close to peace around here. But I really have no idea.

I just don't want to make any big mistakes and cost men their lives and I want to move slowly so we don't go barging in and kill a bunch of innocent people."

"General Hartwick, not only are you a General, you are a damn good one." Schock said.

"Thank you sir."

"The reason I'm calling, is that we want you to know the U.S. military is not going to be involved in this civil war. We are calling you, and we are also trying to reach the California resistance and even the Detroit fighters. We know your NFA is improving its weapons and that's fine. But if chemical, biological, or nuclear type devices of any kind are used we will step in."

"I understand that sir. And I will make sure we don't use such devices. At this point, nothing like that has been considered." Hartwick said.

"Okay. Since we have that out of the way I was wondering if I could ask you a few more questions."

"Sure."

"What are the issues you are fighting for? Because when you took Indianapolis we thought you guys were just going to go back to your lives. I know that spiraled out of your control. But why did you help in Cincinnati and then ultimately St. Louis.

If you were just fighting against the resistance, and to get things back to normal, why the fight with the rebels? And now I know that you are in Michigan. So I'm assuming your fighting against the Muslims in Detroit.

Are you going to join the fight in opposition to the Muslims? I just want to understand what it is you're fighting for."

"To be honest with you Admiral Shock, it's kind of evolved. We did fight to take Indianapolis back. When we saw what the resistance had done there, and when we saw that the politicians had abandoned their posts, we went to help in Cincinnati. Then it just kind of grew from there."

"I understand that General Hartwick. But what is your end goal? What issues are you fighting for?"

"Sir that's evolving as well. It's just in the last few weeks that we realized we may be victorious and we've started to document what we want.

To put it in its simplest terms, we want it to be the way it used to be. And that's not nostalgia and it's not racism.

We just want the country like it was when our dads grew up. Where a man could get a decent job. Pay for a house and pay for college for a kid or two. And if a kid didn't want to go to college, if a kid wanted to work with his hands, well that was okay too. He could still afford to raise a family.

And you'd be surprised Admiral, but a lot of the women who support us feel the same way. They don't want to be looked down on for raising kids and staying home. But too often they can't afford that. So they have to work."

"How do you think you can get there?" Admiral Shock asked.

"We think things were better when we didn't let so many people in the country. Our plan would stop immigration for a generation or two. We think there should be tariffs to protect jobs. We think the government should either fix healthcare, or get out of it. We think there should be a balanced budget amendment and a cap on income taxes.

But we're not just pro-business either. We don't think a corporation in a social media business or manufacturing should be able to control information.

A news network should be owned by the company that owns only news channels. That way they have to make a profit in that business. They can't use the business to spread propaganda. If someone owns a platform that is free to post on, they can't censor the content.

I don't know it all. Like I said we're putting it together and some of it we debate. But essentially we want freedom, and not a security blanket, but a little security that we can get decent jobs."

Then Admiral said nothing for a long time. "That sounds fairly reasonable."

"Well, thank you." Hartwick answered.

"Hartwick?"

"Yes Admiral."

"Don't try to take Detroit. I'm not going to send troops, but I will give you some information. Our satellites show they have a lot of soldiers in there. There are nearly a million men willing to fight.

The blacks and the Muslims aren't fighting against each other in there. Not yet at least. Don't go in there right now. You should have some success pushing in and closing around the loops. But you're going to have to let food in and leave them alone. You can't beat them with what you have now."

"Thank you Admiral. I'll take it under advisement."

"Hartwick don't do it. It will be a disaster. It's twenty times at least what the rebels had. And they have more guns, bombs and other weapons. Promise me you'll wait until you hear from me again. And it could be months."

"I promise you I'll do my absolute best sir." Hartwick said.

"There's one other thing. The politicians here in D.C. aren't going to get it figured out. They aren't going to come to some compromise. At least I don't believe they will.

What that means for you General Hartwick is this. You need to plan for victory. The biggest mistake politicians make during war is failing to prepare for the victory.

Don't make that mistake. Start thinking about it. It may take you a few years. It may happen in months.

The resistance may grow and you could lose. But I doubt it. We've run simulations like this for years. There are very few paths for the left to win. Without the armed forces, hell even with them, there are very few paths for the establishment to hold Washington D.C., much less the entire nation.

You're closer than you think. But it won't be easy. Prepare for victory."

"I'll do that sir." Hartwick said.

"General Hartwick, you'll hear from me again, I promise. And God speed General."

"Thank you sir."

"What did he want?" Evans said.

"He said don't attack Detroit, we can't win. He said we should push into 270 and just hold that. He also said we had to let food in or it would get worse."

"How does he know that?"

"He said they had satellite surveillance. He also said..."

His phone buzzed again. It was a 202 number from D.C. again. But the number was different.

"General Hartwick speaking."

"General it's the admiral again. That first call was official and that number is good if you ever need to call me. But the call will be monitored. So just say something innocuous or ask me for an update on surveillance and I'll call you back on another phone. This phone is a one-off disposable. And this is off the record.

Something is brewing in D.C. I don't know what, and I don't think anyone does. But there is a big change coming. Forget California. It's a lost cause. Contain Detroit and bypass Chicago. Cleveland you could take, but I'd let it go as well.

Once you get Detroit tied down just keep securing everything else and prepare for the east coast.

That's where the battle will be. You'll need a million men well-armed and well trained. We're getting defections from the left as well. It will be ugly. They are forming a perimeter but the bulk of the biggest force you will face will be in Richmond.

I don't know when it will happen. But they are already building up. It might be a year or two. So you have time. Prepare for that battle. Before you get to Richmond, make sure you hold the areas one hundred miles out.

This next part is important. Cut off the internet going into and around Richmond. Then cut down or disable the cell phone towers. If you can, sneak men in and cut off the power in the city. This is going to take a lot of planning and organization. But keep it to just a few people. No more than ten.

Don't let the plan leak. If you take Richmond you'll be primed to take D.C.

When you do that, the generals and admirals will surrender to you and the war will be over. Watch carefully who you trust."

Just as abruptly as the conversation started it ended. Admiral Shock just hung up the phone.

"Now what?" Evans asked.

Hartwick stared at his phone. Should he tell Evans?

"I'll tell you later. For right now we've got to get these guys organized. We need to slowly push in but not cross the loop of 275 or 65. We also need to let food in like he said. We just need to contain them."

"Are you sure you can trust that guy?"

"I don't know. But I think so. A lot of what he said made sense. Once we contain Detroit we need to get back to Indianapolis and meet with Jake Stahl."

"Why?" Evans asked again.

"You'll just have to trust me."

Hartwick and Evans stayed in Michigan for two weeks. They worked the phones and brought troops in to assist. They made plans to contain the city. But they made it clear that the NFA was not to take Detroit no matter what.

The fighting in small towns and rural areas towards the loop was sometimes easy, sometimes hard. But they slowly made progress. By the end of summer, Detroit was sealed in.

There were fierce arguments about letting food in. But Hartwick got them to allow it. Medicine and other necessities were also let in.

Hartwick had to fight passionately for this win. It was incredibly difficult because when he was asked why, he couldn't give them a straight answer.

It was the credibility he had earned from his victory in St. Louis and other places that allowed his word to hold. They were to let small groups of people out if they made it.

They were only to allow Muslims in. Hartwick didn't know if this was the right choice or not. But it was a decision he made and stuck with.

When he realized that his credibility came through St. Louis, and that victory in St. Louis came from Evans he decided he could trust him. When they left for their return trip to Indianapolis he insisted the two drive alone.

He was surprised to learn that Evans was largely in agreement with the Admiral.

They were also in agreement that Jake Stahl, who was now governor of Indiana, and Matt Davis would be in on the plan. Beyond that, they would need time.

As they drove they formulated plans for Richmond. And then Hartwick brought up the other part of Shock's statement.

"He also said we should prepare for victory. Do you have any idea what he meant by that?" Hartwick asked.

"I think it means we have to prepare to rule if we win. The day we win, you realize we will be controlling the entire United States government. I guess we should have a plan for that."

"How?" Hartwick asked.

"Shit I don't know John. You're the general. I guess just start organizing people to run the government and have a plan to do it. You're the best I've ever seen at organizing shit. You and Davis both. You two do that and add anyone who you need. At least that part doesn't have to be secret."

"And the attack on Richmond?" Hartwick asked.

"I know a few men I can absolutely one hundred percent trust. The truth is, we can probably trust most of them. They aren't going to purposefully leak, it's just that people like to talk. It's not going to be easy. We're going to have to figure out a way to pay these guys. We need a professional army."

CHAPTER 11

AUGUST IN THE FREE NATION OF
CALIFORNIA.

Colby Ohlbinger had called for a meeting in Sacramento. The governor would be there as would several state senators and representatives.

He had also insisted the governors of Oregon and Washington attend. And they of course had obliged. Scotch Anderson and several other business leaders were in attendance as well.

Ohlbinger made them wait. He sat in a room next to the large Capitol conference room chatting with his inner circle. The real power brokers. They chatted easily. The group had grown. Over the months Colby had formed close relationships with most of them. When he delegated power to them, he did so unconditionally.

"Are we all set in D.C.?" He asked.

"The plan is set to go into effect in four hours. We have people in twenty offices from California representatives, one senator of course, and three more reps from Oregon and Washington." Gene Strickland had answered.

Strickland was a former college professor. Nearly sixty years old he was well loved and incredibly radical.

Colby liked him immensely but had been forced to pay him nearly a million dollars to leave his tenured job and join the inner circle full time. He believed in the cause of not just socialism, but social justice. Killing for the greater good was to him necessary, and in fact heroic. Even the dead had made a great sacrifice that would benefit their children and grandchildren.

Since the death of Steve Oxley and his admission to the governor, Scotch Anderson and the others in that room so many months ago, Colby began to question the killings. He knew it was sometimes necessary. What would take place today was necessary. But he began to wish that it were not.

"What's the total number?" He asked.

"Sixty people." Strickland answered. I believe that's correct isn't it Katana?"

Katana was growing weary of everything. Colby knew he had to get her out fast. "Yeah. Sixty people. They're all armed and ready to go." And now I have to go.

She stood up and left the room without another word. Most figured she was just like that. A bit anti-social. Colby knew better. She was done.

When she had left Colby scanned the room. He liked this new style of leadership. It was very democratic. If he needed to settle an argument he would do it. If he really wanted something, he would get it. But he found he was actually earning more respect by listening and delegating power.

Things were going well in California. The right had been largely banished. The ones that remained realized free healthcare and a higher minimum wage had actually worked. Now was the time to expand.

"So are we still all in agreement? No last minute defections?"

No one spoke. "I mean this. Guys, you have to tell me now. If you don't think we're ready, we can hold off. I think we're ready. I think things are going well and with the trouble in St. Louis and now Detroit this is the time. But I am open to any debate at all."

"No Colby, we've talked this thing to death now. We're all ready and we're all on board. The Free Nation of California, well, Oregon and Washington as well, is long overdue. I've worked my entire life for this and I think I speak for all of us; it is time." Strickland answered.

"And if the politicians in there and the business leaders object?" Colby asked.

"Stick to the plan my boy, stick to the wonderful plan Strickland answered.

Colby looked around the room. "Everyone okay?"

Most just nodded. Some gave a thumbs up and a few smiled and answered in the affirmative.

"Gene, you sure you don't want to go in there with me? I'm fine with going by myself. I sometimes prefer it. But I don't want to leave you out."

"No, no, my boy. I prefer the concrete myself. I'll stay behind the scenes and do the math and other heavy lifting. You're very good at the politics of the whole mess. You handle that then right?"

Colby just nodded.

"Okay then. Go get them. If they won't go along, force the issue and tell them the people want this and their voices must be heard."

Colby nodded again. He smiled and left the room. "When I get back we'll be in a new nation."

When he walked into the conference room they all stood up and applauded. It had been weeks since they'd last met. As politicians and other assorted suck ups, they were accustomed to false praise. Colby graciously thanked them and asked them to sit. He didn't like the fake fawning.

As they were sitting, he could see that at the far end of the table, Scotch Anderson had not stood to applaud. He shook his head slightly and said to himself, 'I own that guy, doesn't matter anyway'.

"I've called this meeting to address a few things. We've been circulating among the people and taken a few polls (Everyone in the room knew this was not true. Colby knew they knew it was not true, but everyone played the game) the people want this. We are confident in that. And we think it's time to make a significant move."

Almost everyone in the group moved to the edge of their seats. Colby noticed Anderson had not. He was slumped in his chair twiddling his pen in his fingers. Perhaps it had been a mistake to invite him after all.

"The country is now divided. War rages in the Midwest and the south. But here it becomes more peaceful every day. We believe, the people believe, that it is time we secede. It is time we formed our own nation."

There was silence in the room. Colby wanted their approval. He knew the politicians still held sway over the states. He wasn't sure they realized this, and he wasn't sure they had the backbone to resist. But he wanted their support.

"Any thoughts?"

It was Scotch Anderson who finally spoke.

"How?" He asked.

"I'm sorry Scotch, what do you mean?"

"I mean how? I don't want to be disrespectful, I don't want any more trouble. But how are you going to do this?"

Colby noticed the 'more trouble' in Anderson's sentence.

"Well, we've had Gene Strickland and some of the other professors in the group look into that. They tell me we just need to inform our representatives in D.C., notify the Congress, and the President, and that's that. The representatives would all come home and be representatives here."

"What do we use for money? How do we trade with them? I mean the first thing we would need to do is establish a currency. How do we trade with other nations? Do we still trade with the Midwest?

Because that's where a lot of our food and oil comes from. And more importantly, the food we grow brings in money to the state by selling it to them."

"Well, we can keep using the dollar. And yes, if we can, we of course trade with the farmers and manufacturers in the Midwest. And remember the east coast is still siding more with us than the right." Colby answered.

"Okay. If you're going to use the dollar, are we still sending federal taxes to Washington D.C.?" Anderson asked.

"Of course not. Why would we? We will have our own nation. Look, I hear it all the time, we send them more money than they send back to the state anyway. Why would we continue to do that?" Colby answered

"Because that's largely a myth. What we get in return is a guarantee on our bonds. We issue debt and the U.S. government backs it. If we don't send taxes to them they won't accept our dollars. They'll just change the currency or close us off from the Fed."

Colby was in over his head. He was beginning to wonder if Scotch was right.

"I'm sorry Scotch, I really am. This is not my area of expertise. Let me just check with Strickland real quick. He has assured me this is all good to go, but I want to get the details. I'll be right back."

"Don't bother." Anderson said. "Strickland is an idiot. Do you know he makes over six-hundred thousand dollars a year as a professor of history? Do you know that he hasn't taught a class in about thirty years? And that he continues to receive his pay?

He taught Marxism, that's it. He was allowed to stop teaching because people were complaining that he just ranted for hours on end. So they promoted him. He knows nothing and he will have no answers for you."

"All the same, I think I'd like to bring him in."

Colby left the room and rushed to Strickland. "You have to go in there with me. They are talking about bonds and monetary policy and I don't know what to tell them."

He noticed Strickland stiffen and go momentarily pale. He recomposed himself quickly. He had no intention of entering the conference room. He faked a broad smile. "Oh my boy how I would love to go in there. Let me guess, it's one of the business owners who is objecting right?"

"Well, yes, it is." Colby answered.

"Oh how I envy you Colby my boy. He's just talking in circles. Don't let him frustrate you. We'll have our own currency and we'll be fine. It takes a bit of time, not much. During the transition, it can get a little bad for a spell but it passes quickly. No, I believe I'll leave the joy of beating them over the head intellectually to the younger people. You've earned it. Just tell him we know it will take a spot of time but we will be just fine."

Colby went back into the room and told him what Strickland had said.

"See Colby? He said nothing. He sent you back in here with no real advice. Look, Colby, I want to help you. I do. Not because I like you or I think you're right. I don't. But you did tell the truth about one thing. Us. We did this to you.

Every movie you saw growing up and every television show you watched did this. They were crafted to get you to think a certain way. It worked. We thought it would give us more power and money.

If we could get you to hate Republicans, and think they were racist bigots, we would have you. If we could get you to believe they were stealing from you, we would have you. We could work with the Democrats. We could give you free stuff and make you feel better.

Then they would pass laws giving us cheap labor and at the same time make it harder for small business to grow and compete with us. We did this, and it got out of hand.

I take my share of responsibility for that. But I also won't lie to myself again. This is a bad idea. It is a terrible idea in fact. And now I have told you why. I cannot force you to listen. All I can do is tell you the truth. And I will do my best to give you good advice to make this work if you do secede. But I seriously doubt it will work."

Colby was frustrated and angry. Anderson was right about Strickland. But that didn't mean Strickland was wrong about everything. Something inside him wanted to make Anderson believe. For some reason he could not articulate to himself, he wanted Anderson on his side.

He had an idea. He thought it might backfire, but he had to try something. He was beginning to understand these people. He believed that they had lied to him and everyone else. But he thought he might just be able to make that right as well.

"Look Scotch, and everyone else here, I want you to listen to me closely. We are learning. We are beginning to understand what it is you want. And we agree with you to an extent. Scotch, no one is going to take your business away from you. In fact, your taxes will probably fall once we stop sending money to Washington. We want to control the energy sector and we want the public to own health care. Top to bottom.

Strickland has made it clear we are going to have to force people to work. But with a good wage, they will want too. We are not against any of you. We don't want communism. Well, not all of us anyway. We want a social safety net like they have in Sweden or Germany.

You will own your business and we will leave you alone."

"You can have my business. Without the rule of law, without a constitution like the United State Constitution, you will be able to take it any time you want. So take it now. I do not care. I will help you. But I won't lie to myself ever again. If you want it, it is yours. And I will still help. Only because I helped to create this fucking mess." Anderson said.

He then looked around the room. No one else had spoken. The businessmen were either terrified or satisfied, he could not tell. The politicians were terrified. He knew this was over. They were going to secede. It didn't matter what he said. So Anderson continued to talk.

"So, why don't we all take a vote? Is anyone opposed to secession of California, Oregon and Washington into the Peoples Republic of California?"

He asked. No one responded.

"So there you have it Colby. Complete political cover. Now, who is the president of this great new nation? Or do we have one?"

Ohlbinger was stunned. It had been too easy. "Uh, well we thought the governors would continue in their role and our committee would lead until we could have elections. Which we would hope would be very soon. Oh, and we are calling it the Free Nation of California."

"So is that it for today?" Anderson asked.

"If there are no questions or other business, I guess so."

When the meeting ended Colby returned to the adjacent meeting room. Strickland was still there but most of the others had left.

"How did it go my boy?" Strickland asked.

Colby was agitated. With just three people in the room, he felt like he could, and should challenge the professor. He was only fifty-eight or fifty-nine years old, but he acted like he was eighty. He was born and raised in California, but faked a slight English accent. His arrogance had to be checked.

The professor had to be put in his place. But he was also nervous about it. The others really seemed to like him.

If Anderson was right, and this turned into a disaster, he knew the people would turn on him as quickly as they turned to him.

He needed to get the national police force in place. He hated the idea, but again Strickland had been persuasive. There would be problems if it wasn't done. It would be a temporary necessity. He decided to push back on Strickland.

"Are you sure about this currency thing Strickland?" Colby normally referred to him as Gene or Professor. He wanted to assert some authority over the arrogant man.

"Getting cold feet my boy?" Strickland asked.

"Not at all. But, I've trusted you on a lot of the details. Are you sure about this? We are all counting on you. You wanted to take the ball on the reconstruction. Surely you don't mind me asking for a few of the details?"

He tried to say it as nicely as possible but he was afraid it had come out contentious or confrontational. So he smiled.

"Colby, this is nothing new. Nations have done this for hundreds of years. As I said before, it can be a little rocky at the start. That's one of the reasons you need a loyal, well paid national police force. But if you get people to work, and give them some security, they'll quickly accept the new currency."

Colby let it go. When he was alone he realized that once again Strickland hadn't really said anything. He made a point to schedule a one on one meeting with Scotch Anderson. It was a critical moment for the movement. He had to get good advice. He didn't want to lose it all now. But first, he had to let this afternoon play out.

It was noon in Washington D.C. In just three more hours his plans would either be solidified or fall apart quickly. He rushed to his next meeting.

When he opened his hotel room door Katana was already there. Two other people were there as well. Both confidants of Katana and both young men who knew exactly what was going to go down in D.C.

"How confident are you guys?" He wanted to ask Katana directly but she had been so quiet lately that he just threw the question out.

Justin Ternau was just as aggressive as Katana but much more passionate and willing to talk.

"It's all set. Congress passing a law to allow staffers to carry guns in the Capitol is probably the dumbest thing they ever did." Ternau said.

"So all sixty have guns?" Colby asked, knowing the answer already.

"Well, no. Only thirty-five or so were able to pass the background check. But those that do each have two guns. So by the time it starts, all of our people will be armed. The joint session lets out at three O'clock. Should be a full house. That's five hundred and thirty-five people counting the senators.

We are only targeting Republicans. If we can take out two-hundred, we should be able to take control."

"So each shooter has to get three kills and a few more have to get four kills if my math is right." Ohlbinger offered.

"That's what we're hoping. We know there will be some collateral. But we feel confident that the Capitol police will be slow to react and lost in the confusion. Even if we only get one hundred and fifty, we think we can still take control. We have another few hundred stationed outside the city ready to storm in when it's time."

"You'll be lucky to get fifty." Katana said.

"What?" Ternau protested. "We have sixty people. There are ten rounds in each gun. That's six hundred rounds that are going to be fired. Katana, I'm pretty sure even the bad shots can get three kills out of ten shots.

Even if they don't, the three hundred outside will be storming the steps before the ambulances even arrive. They will mop up, and we'll take control."

Katana just shook her head and smiled. "You're so fucking stupid Justin. You really are.

First, only about half of those sixty will fire. The rest will run. Of the thirty that fire, half of them will be shooting into the air. So you might get fifteen people shooting accurately. Let's say you're right and they get three kills. That means forty-five. And that's your best case."

"Well, Katana, even if you're right, when the three-hundred storm the steps they're going to get a few kills as well don't you think? So half of them each get one kill. Now you're at almost two-hundred. Just like I said."

Colby listened to the two. He wanted to believe Ternau. He believed Katana.

"Can we still take the Capitol?" He asked Katana.

She hedged for a second and looked at the ceiling while thinking.

When Colby and Katana had first met she was forty pounds overweight, but much of that muscle. Her hair was streaked with pink and blue. She had piercings in her nose and lips. She wore old gray sweat suits.

Now her hair was her natural light brown. She had lost nearly fifty pounds. She wore tight-fitting blue jeans and sleeveless shirts. She wore no makeup and Colby realized she was actually quite attractive. She rarely smiled and even less rarely spoke.

"I don't see how." She said.

"So what the hell is the point of all of this?" Colby said. He was trying not to yell at her. She had been on board with the plan from the start.

"The point is to disrupt. If this works at all, if you get even one or two kills it will cause disruption. Then the right wingers will leave us alone. California, Oregon and Washington will be allowed to secede. No one will bother us. But don't kid yourselves. None of our people will get out alive." She said.

Colby had a sudden realization.

"You knew this from the start. That's why you didn't let the Rebecca girl go isn't it?" He said.

Katana nodded slightly.

"She doesn't know this for sure. Ternau protested. She can't see the fucking future. This is a solid plan. Look, it may not go perfectly. But all we have to do is create enough chaos to get our three-hundred in and take control. When that happens ten thousand more will come every day and we'll have the nation. Then we can force the Army to fight with us."

Colby knew this was ridiculous. But if they could take control of the Capitol building for just a few weeks maybe they could win. The army would never fight, he knew that, the admiral had told him. But that could also work to their advantage.

Somewhere between Katana and Justin Ternau was the truth. He hoped it was closer to Ternau. But even if they only killed forty-five people, it could still work.

They ordered pizza, turned on the television and waited.

At three O'clock they moved to the edge of their seats. The anchor was talking about the special joint session of Congress that was ending.

The scene moved to inside the Capitol building and the remote reporter was speaking. As the doors opened she rushed to the first person she could find. It was a Democrat from Vermont. She asked them if any issues had been resolved and what transpired.

Others were walking and smiling in the background. There was no gunfire. There was no chaos.

After a few minutes they realized nothing would transpire. Katana stood up. Laughed, and left the room. After a few more minutes Colby looked at Justin. "I guess Katana was right."

Just as he said it a few pops could be heard, and people in the building started running. The camera panned around and was shaking. Then the feed cut.

At the anchor desk the talking heads were scrambling. Clearly something had happened and they were fairly certain they had heard gunfire.

"Oh yeah?" Ternau said.

Colby kept staring at the television waiting for news. A few minutes later the remote reporter at the Capitol building was back.

There has been some kind of attack. We are not sure what is going on but a group tried to rush the Capitol building."

"Has anyone inside been injured?" The anchor desk reporter asked.

"No, all are safe in here. Our cameraman tried to get a look outside but the doors were quickly closed."

"Oh no." Colby said.

"What? What's going on?" Justin screamed.

Colby just looked at him. "Don't you get it? The three-hundred are starting the second wave. But because there was no first wave there was no confusion. They were spotted by the police and are being stopped at the steps."

Colby walked to the television and turned it off.

"Go home Justin. It's over."

It would be several more hours before Colby knew what had happened. Because of the Joint Session, there was to be extra security. They had decided to ban all guns in the building for the day.

The three-hundred attackers had not known this, and had proceeded as planned. Katana had been right. Only two-hundred or so showed up. They were spotted before they ever got close to the steps.

Colby sat alone in his hotel room. There were bodies lying at the front of the Capitol in the street. More were scattered about. On top of that news the reporters were talking about California, Oregon and Washington seceding from the union.

They were speculating that the two events were connected. Colby's phone buzzed constantly. He told the reporters he was not aware of any connection and that he was busy going about the business of helping to govern the new nation. There would be a press conference and the 'foreign press' from the United States would be welcomed to attend.

After four interviews he had simply stopped answering his phone. He knew this was a loss. Not only had they gained no influence or control in D.C., their representatives and staffs would now be sent home because they had seceded. Information about what was going on would now be harder to get.

But in some small way, he knew the sacrifice would be worth it. The deaths of the three-hundred would cause enough of a distraction to focus on building the Free Nation of California.

Strickland had suggested that the next move should be to build an army to secure the nation and strike east. They had made plans to take Nevada, Arizona, New Mexico and Colorado, but they knew it would have to wait until next spring.

But Ohlbinger had seen enough. His mission would be to hold on to their gains. He would work with Anderson and anyone else to create a Scandinavian type nation for the West Coast. In his group there were committed communists and socialists. But he knew the answer was somewhere in between.

On the television the governor of California was being interviewed. She expressed sympathy at the violence in Washington and expressed optimism for the future.

Colby knew he had to lead. He wanted to lead. But something was changing in him. With victory at hand he was having doubts. He knew he needed help. And he would take advice. But he wouldn't let them bully him into abandoning the cause. They wanted socialism. He wanted socialism. He would deliver.

He would bridge the gap between the business owners, the communists and the politicians.

The first step was to solidify control and the victory. He would order a national holiday for Monday. No one but the most essential would be allowed to work. Businesses would be forced to pay their employees for the day off.

Then he would announce the elections. His committee would rule with the governors for the first year. Then there would be open elections. Everyone was allowed to vote. Everyone over the age of eighteen, maybe even sixteen.

He would head the committee. A nation needed a President. He would tell them it was just a title. Someone had to be a single point of contact to establish trade deals and treaties with foreign nations. He would act as President, but only for a short time.

Then he would build the army to defend the gains. There were going to be tough months ahead. But he had won. He was the head of one of the most powerful nations in the world. Not yet thirty-two years old, and he was a world leader.

Failure was not an option. He gathered his small security detail from the adjoining rooms. He would need to pay them more. They should be the highest paid employees in the state. That would keep them loyal. And he would need more of them.

He marched out of the hotel with his detail and across the street to the Capitol building. Today the city of Sacramento would become the Capital of the nation of California.

And Colby Ohlbinger would be the first President.

CHAPTER 12

THE LONG WINTER

Fall turned to winter and the nation was generally peaceful. The United States technically existed as it always had except for California, Oregon and Washington.

But even the remaining states were not united.

The Midwest, the south and the northwest were isolated from New England. Virginia itself was divided with Richmond clearly in the sphere of D.C.

Pennsylvania was divided from Philadelphia to everything to the west of the city. In Detroit, the Muslim radicals had seceded, but the moderates still fought and the city was surrounded by a small army.

The first of the winter fights were small but decisive. Hartwick's army of the right was winning the middle of the country.

In Sacramento, Colby worked with the leadership committee. He was the President, but yielded as much power as he thought he could while still maintaining control.

The new government was now paying its army and trying to solidify Oregon and repel attacks in Olympia, Seattle, and Washington.

In early December both would fall. The NFA troops, now solidly united under Hartwick and led by Tory Evans and a growing group of military professionals, pushed quickly on Tacoma and set up a new government.

The state had officially rejoined the union. Yet the structure was not traditional.

In the East Coast states, taxes continued to flow to D.C. In the state of Washington, the new government would follow the Indiana model. The federal taxes collected would be held by the state. Money was sent to D.C. to pay for social security, Medicare, the military and nothing else.

States were free to do whatever they wanted, but most had followed the Indiana model set up by Jake Stahl.

State spending was cut drastically. Welfare was gone and the homeless and those living in housing paid for by the state were rounded up and pushed into old hotels.

"Don't starve let them starve, and keep a roof over their heads. But don't let them get comfortable." Was Stahl's motto.

The only thing that Hartwick pushed states to do was fund a military.

The volunteer army had worked in the early months. But desertions were common and training was nearly impossible. Florida would not follow. They sent all due taxes to the Federal Government and kept their welfare systems in place.

Texas had decided on the Indiana model. Illinois tried to follow Florida's lead, but the fighting in Chicago made it largely irrelevant. Nearly half of the state was simply run by Indiana. What state government that was left in Illinois tried to fix Chicago.

When the state of Washington fell there was a push into Oregon. The state quickly divided with the eastern two-thirds joining

Washington and the western counties, now controlled by an army from California held to the new nation.

So it began. The three nations of winter. On the East Coast, a clear line from just south of Richmond Virginia was in all but name, its own nation. The rest of the states in the center of country were another nation, loosely aligned with the East Coast.

On the west coast was the official Free Nation of California. The nation also consisted of one-third of Oregon. Each of the three sections was for the most part peaceful. And each had areas where there was little or no control.

In California, San Diego was still in a constant state of war. Ohlbinger and his government had tried to take the city and bring the large naval base under control. Neither would surrender.

There was no fighting around the Naval base or other small military bases. But they were guarded well and defended. Desertions on the bases were over thirty percent. But more than enough remained to hold.

The rest of the state was not only peaceful but economic activity was growing quickly. The port of Los Angeles was particularly busy. The products delivered across the Pacific Ocean still had to be distributed. For the privilege of using the port the new nation of California was levying a heavy tax.

They would spend the coming months holding Oregon and solidifying California into a robust and viable nation. The leaders of the new nation would plan for the spring as well. It was clear a battle was coming. Their mission was to hold on to their gains and grow slowly where they could.

In the states in the center of the nation, there were still protests but they were peaceful and often broken up quickly. The area around Detroit was the exception.

On the East Coast there was also division. Two things were clear to the establishment government in Washington D.C.

The first was that an attack was coming. The second was that California was working to build a large defense force.

The military was still committed to staying out of the conflict. But President Hoxworth and the Republicans were also aware that the bureaucrats were largely working with the left.

Money was flowing to this new establishment army. Many were professional security for The Environmental Protection Agency, The IRS, and the Social Security Administration. They were not named and not acknowledged by the Democrats or the Republicans.

Some were paid directly by the government. They were given titles and jobs. They were janitorial staff, human resources specialists, information technology technicians, and thousands of other made up titles. They were in fact soldiers.

Republicans went along with this hoping it would preserve the union until an agreement could be arranged with the middle of the country.

The establishment east coast army stretched from Watertown New York, at the very northern edge of the state, all the way to just south of Richmond Virginia.

They knew from spies and other friendlies in the middle of the nation that John Hartwick was planning something to the east.

They did not know where an attack would come, but they were certain that something was coming.

The establishment army was stretched all along Interstate eighty-one. Just to the southern edge of D.C., the line followed sixty-six east back to ninety-95. From there it followed south to Richmond.

North of Richmond, the line bulged along 295. The loop around the city. When they tried to move outside of this boundary they encountered resistance and pulled back.

Along I-81 the stretch between Hagerstown and Winchester was the most heavily guarded. This area offered the quickest path to Washington D.C. and thus was considered the most vulnerable area.

Troy Evans, John Hartwick, Jake Stahl, Matt Davis, and six other people knew the attack was going to be on Richmond.

Hartwick and Evans had travelled south to bring in the eleventh and twelfth members of the inner group who would know where the attack would be.

The final two members were critically important to their success. The first was Roy Desmond. The governor of Texas. The second was John Robert Ross. The famous evangelical preacher operating out of Dallas Texas.

From the first days of violence, all eyes had been on Texas. For a few weeks, the protests had been violent in Austin. But the rioters and protesters had been rounded up quickly and thrown in jail. There had been no more than small protests since. Those were confined to Dallas and Houston and had also been quickly brought under control.

Even the Senators and congressional representatives from Texas thought the state would secede first. But it had not happened. Two men had stopped it.

Roy Desmond, the second term governor, had argued that Texas should stay with the union and work to stop the violence.

John Robert Ross, the evangelical preacher, had appealed to the Christian faith of the citizens of Texas to avoid violence. It was a pair of men that would be hard to stop.

Jake Stahl had contacted Governor Desmond just two months ago, and Desmond had quickly agreed to join the center states in withholding a chunk of federal income taxes. He would commit to nothing more.

"Governor Desmond we want to tell you what our plan for the future is." Hartwick said.

"We believe that California is a lost cause. We also believe that what we are seeing on the east coast is a mirage. We don't think they are as united as it would appear. We have a very high-level contact in the military who thinks that we need to make a move militarily. But he tells us the government military will not help."

"So Admiral Shock has talked to you eh? Well, I thought that might be the case. I know he wants you to make a run on Richmond. Is that still the plan?" Desmond answered.

Troy Evans and Hartwick showed the obvious confusion on their faces. "Wait, so Shock contacted you too? How many people know about this?" Evans asked.

"How many people have you two told?" The governor asked.

"Eight more. We thought we were the only ones." Hartwick said.

"Well, I'm guessing that eleven know. Because I knew he called you General Hartwick. But he told me I was the only other one he had told of the idea. You know, The Admiral and I go way back.

In fact, just a few days before you guys called I was planning on calling you. I'm a Navy guy. I don't know if you know that. And this is a land war. But Shock thought if I could get Texas behind you, we might just pull this off.

In Texas, all of the military bases have made it clear they support Texas first. That caused us to lose quite a few soldiers. It also caused quite a few more to get mysteriously transferred here.

The reason Admiral Shock called me is that he and his fellow leaders in the military believe that Texas needs to be the last line of defense.

We have an agreement with them. We will help you in any way we can short one thing. We can't let the military men fight. We'll help with guns, and we'll turn a blind eye to any instruction they might give you. No explosives, tanks or any other heavy equipment.

We'll help you get men to fight with you. But your soldiers from Texas have to be civilians.

I think you can count on at least a few hundred thousand men. That sound good?"

Hartwick and Evans both smiled and nodded. "That sounds great Governor. But we have one more favor to ask. Maybe more than a favor it's just advice.

"Fire away." Desmond said.

"We want to talk to John Robert Ross. That TV preacher from Dallas. We'd like him to give us moral support." Hartwick said.

"He's really popular here in Texas gentlemen. He's probably the biggest reason we didn't have much of a problem here. But before you do that, you need to know a little more about him."

The governor paused before continuing. He pulled a cigarette from his pocket and lit it.

"You fellas mind if I smoke?" He asked.

"Hell its war." Evans said. Everybody smokes during war, don't they? Can I bum one from you?"

"I'll take one too if you don't mind." Hartwick added after a sheepish glance at Evans.

Desmond gave them both cigarettes, and as the room filled with smoke he began to talk about John Robert Ross.

"You guys just see JR on television or listen to him on the radio. You probably think he is one of those prosperity preachers who just tells people what they want to here. Then he makes a ton of money and gets famous.

"I like him. I think he does a lot of good. I listen to him on the radio a couple of times a week. I think he's great." Evans said.

"I like him too." Hartwick said. "I think people obviously like him and listen to him.

But I do think he is a prosperity preacher. I really do. But I don't care. He does a good thing and I think he helps bring the country together."

"Gentlemen, the truth is, John Robert Ross is a deeply religious man. The reason we didn't have big problems down here is that he has a huge following. And the people that go to his church are white, black, Mexican, Asian, and any other thing you can think of. He wants people to do well and be happy. But he is also a man who believes in the bible. He thinks violence is a sin.

Now that doesn't mean he won't help. But you're going to have to explain why you are doing this and let him make up his own mind. If he thinks you are doing something wrong, not only won't he help you, he'll work against you."

When the governor had finished talking he snuffed out his cigarette and picked up the phone.

"JR? Hey it's Roy. I have a couple of friends from Indiana who would like to have dinner with you. Can you make time for them tomorrow?"

The meeting was set just that easily. When John Robert Ross was given a promise that both men would work hard to stop any kind of forced emigration for blacks, Hispanics or any other group, he agreed to help. He gave his word he would not leak the plans and would say nothing until just before the battle was to begin.

At that point he would rally the nation behind Hartwick's New Freedom Army. But he would also deliver a sermon on moral conduct during war.

When they returned to Indiana they continued planning and organizing. The media were reporting on the movement of men in large numbers across the Midwest and south.

The East Coast army of volunteers and paid government workers grew by the day.

During the months of January, February and March the entire world knew what was coming. A huge battle for the nation.

CHAPTER 13

RICHMOND

T he southern wing of Hartwick's NFA was gathered at Prince Edward-Gallion State Park in Virginia.

They were fifty miles from their destination, south of Richmond. At Four O'clock in the morning, they began to move out. There were just over one-hundred thousand men. Over twenty-thousand were in trucks.

They would arrive first and secure the area. Behind them, eighty-thousand more would march. In three hour stretches, they would move slowly to the east towards the city.

One-hundred and seventy miles to the north, in the small town of Strasburg Virginia, fifty-thousand of Hartwick's soldiers were moving east. Just sixteen miles to the north, in Winchester, was a growing army from the establishment government forces.

They had expected an attack somewhere along this line marching towards D.C.

The first battle was happening at Cedar Creek and Belle Grove National Historic Park.

Troy Evan's was the senior officer. Their routes of retreat were already well established. As his army moved east men who knew of the plan would move among the army. They were told that it was a diversion only at the last minute.

The government army moved quickly from Winchester to the south to engage. A smaller contingent moved from the south to pinch Evan's troops.

The fighting started in the state park with a few random shots across a valley. Both armies had settled along two ridges with Fort Valley in the center. The armies were stationed four miles away from each other.

Both sides would send small groups of a few hundred into the valley and pitched battles ensued.

Seventy miles to the south another NFA army of one-hundred thousand men was moving east through Stanton Virginia. Troy Evan's mission was to hold as long as he could throughout the day. If there was a charge we would retreat. If there was a lull he would attack.

When he attacked, he would always send men ahead to Interstate 66 towards Washington D.C. Several groups from five-hundred to a thousand or more men would try to draw the government forces into a defensive position along 66 all the way to D.C.

Another group of five thousand was sent north along I-81. There were to shut off the power by destroying transformers and sub-stations. Fiber optic cables were also cut.

By noon the power was out, cell service and internet had been cut to most of the areas north and east of D.C.

In Richmond, the power was on and all was calm. As night began to fall a light mist turned in to a steady rain.

Evan's moved his forces in groups of a few thousand at a time to the south along State Route 11 just along I-81. They knew 81 was guarded. 11 ran parallel and was slower going but easier to avoid detection. They would rally in Staunton Virginia. By morning they would move eighty miles to the east towards Richmond. All along the way Evan's troops would disrupt the line. This drew East Coast troops from the south near Richmond up to him. His feint worked brilliantly

Through the night five-hundred men from the NFA would wreak havoc inside Richmond. Just ten groups of five men, well-armed and well stocked with 'Farmer Footballs', the little bombs they had first used in St. Louis spread throughout the city.

The establishment leaders back in Washington knew what was happening. Communications were slow but they knew Richmond was the target.

There was furious work behind the scenes to stop the East Coast army from getting the information. But it could not be hidden.

President Hoxworth and his advisors worked fruitlessly to get the Democrat's to intercede and withdraw. They would not cooperate.

Hoxworth, Van Driessen, and a handful of Republicans could not persuade the Democrats that they just might lose. President Hoxworth called The Joint Chief's Chairman, Admiral Shock, to make sure the military would not intervene. Once confirmed he tried again to get the left to withdraw again. It did not work.

Thousands of establishment forces were now leaving D.C., Philadelphia and other areas along the 81 line and racing towards Richmond.

At Three o'clock the southern wing of the NFA had made it to the James River. Resistance had been light. They halted for thirty minutes to allow rear troops to catch up.

North of the city in a small town called Smart Pump, tens of thousands of NFA forces were gathered. There had been little resistance and many locals had joined to help attack Richmond and move north to D.C.

At just before Four o'clock everything was in place and the first trucks began to cross the I-95 Bridge into the city.

As the first few trucks crossed the river, gunfire erupted. This slowed the advance and just a few rows back the multi-gun trucks took positions forward. Six of them opened fire across the bridge. The catapult launchers also let loose their Ammonium Nitrate and Diesel bombs.

The middle and rear sections were beginning to cross fourteenth Street, Ninth Street and 301 bridges into the city.

As fires and explosions ignited across the river, the I-95 Bridge exploded. Bombs had been placed underneath and all along the bridge and on ramps.

Jacob Picket, the retired marine Colonel, had been put in charge of Hartwick's southern Army. He was sixty years old but still maintained his Marine regimen. He was just to the east of the bridge trying to create a temporary communication center as the bridge exploded. He watched as thousands of his men fell to their deaths in the river.

Fearing the other bridges would be bombed as well he quickly rerouted his forces and multi-guns well to the west towards Westover Hills bridge and the toll bridge just a few miles away.

Maymont was on the other side. Much less populated and offering open fields to the east and good cover to the west his troops crossed easily and established a foothold.

To the north, Evans had moved his forces to the soccer fields and surrounding woods in an area called Bryan's park.

The eastern attack of another hundred thousand men moved through The University of Richmond to a golf course just two and a half miles from Picket's forces.

Richmond was contained from the south to west all the way up to Route 33. But I-95 to the north was wide open and troops from the enemy army could move freely and quickly.

In Maymont, Picket rallied his troops and started to move them towards the city. Evan's army to the north had to move to contain I-95 and stop troops and supplies from reaching the enemy.

The eastern troops, led by two capable men from Texas would press east and support Picket.

The first big battle took place in two cemeteries. Hollywood cemetery and Riverview cemetery. Just short of one mile wide, Picket planned to march around the grave sites out of respect. But he was stopped at I-95 just north of the cemeteries, and forced to hold.

From a residential area on the eastern edge of the fields,
bullets rained down on the NFA troops. They were pushed back to
the edge.

The multi-gun trucks and catapult trucks that hadn't been
lost on the bridge were moved to the front. The first charge was set.

As soon as the trucks started to move, heavier gunfire
erupted and the enemy army of the east unleashed a barrage of
their own explosives. Two of the ten remaining multi-gun trucks
were destroyed and all but one of the catapult launchers as well.

Picket retreated again to the edge and cover. A massive
charge of all of his men would be necessary to make it to the center
of the city and capital of the state.

He watched from a safe distance as men fought to get to
wounded and dead soldiers. It was close to six and the sky was
already getting dark. The fighting had been going on all day.

Ahead of Picket just a few yards, he heard a shot. He looked
up to the top of a two-story apartment building where it had come
from. A young brown haired kid looked down at him and shouted.
"Got another one sir!"

Picket just smiled at the kid. That's good work son. Keep
'em off our boys!"

"Will do sir." The boy said. And turned his attention back to
the scope on his rifle. Just a few seconds later he fired again. "Got
another one sir."

Picket turned to the man next to him. "Who the hell is that
kid?" He asked.

The man smiled and said. "Jimmy Edward Burns, or Jeb as he likes to be called. He says he is eighteen years old. We brought him up from Georgia. His dad swore he was eighteen and had joined the army. He just got out of high school this past year and was set to go to basic in July. But when the fighting broke out, well, he changed his mind I guess."

When the last of the men had been pulled from the cemetery battle field Picket called the kid down.

"You stay with me from now on. You're a great sniper and we might need you for special duty. Also, you're a sergeant now Jeb. That's called a battlefield promotion."

Jeb just smiled and nodded. "Yes sir. Thank you sir. He saluted smartly and walked away.

For the rest of the night Picket would work and organize. They would need to push through the cemetery to the east and then through the residential areas.

Tens of thousands of men were going to have to be quickly organized and pushed harder than they ever had been in their lives. Picket knew what was coming. As men fell dead, others would become afraid and run. It would be a long night.

While Picket was fighting in the south, Evans was pushing fast to the north. He pushed his troops ten miles to the north to I-95 and 295 to stop or slow down new troops from the EA, or establishment army, as the enemy were now being called.

There were two exits not much more than half a mile apart. I-95 was the biggest but State Route 1 just to the west was also an easy path to get EA troops to the city.

Evans rushed in quickly with five-thousand men between and along the two exits. They took the first, the Route 1 exits quickly, and pushed towards the I-95 exit. At the 95 exit they bogged down quickly. Evans moved some of his men to the wooded areas to the north and west. But he couldn't cross the highway because of fierce opposition.

He concentrated nearly half of his troops to the North West corner. They would move in and blow up the overpass. That would slow any movement from the EA.

They made progress moving just a few feet at a time. Evans was in the front and firing as he barked orders to make it to the overpass and set the charges.

Men were dropping all around him. But they held together. There were within just a few feet of their targets when the EA forces suddenly retreated. He ordered men from the high side of the road to follow him and rushed towards the overpass and began to set explosives.

He heard a thump. It was the familiar sound of a mortar canon. He raised his head and saw dozens of canisters flying towards the open area in the center of the loop. He and nearly five hundred other men were working furiously to blow the bridges.

When the canisters hit, smoke started pouring from them. He felt a burning in his nose and eyes. He tried to breathe and the burning went deeply into his lungs.

"Tear gas!" Someone yelled and they tried to keep working. But as the seconds wore on Troy Evans knew this was not just tear gas. Men began vomiting and falling.

He ordered a retreat. He tried to run back to the east but he was becoming disoriented.

He fell to his knees and tried to crawl. A man was laying in front of him twitching. He reached out and grabbed the man by the back of his coat and tried to pull him out. Then the gunfire erupted.

He rose to his feet still trying to pull the man. He felt a bullet go into his back. It was high, near the shoulder. He fell back to his knees.

He tried to stand again and was hit a second time. He fell again and rolled to his back. He raised his head and saw the EA forces jumping from the edges of the overpass firing blindly towards Troy and his troops.

Then the bridge exploded. Troy Evans, the first commissioned officer of the New Freedom Army, was dead. But his mission had been completed.

Hartwick had kissed his wife and children goodbye. It was a strange farewell. He was only going about five miles away. Back to the parking lot where it had all started.

He was smoking a cigarette and standing with his shoulder leaned against the post of a drug store. His phone buzzed.

"General Hartwick?" A voice said. "This is Dave Baxter. I'm, well I work with General Picket. We're here south of the city."

"How's it going?" Hartwick asked.

"Uhh, we're digging in and preparing for the morning. I have some bad news sir. Troy Evans has been killed. He was up to the north fighting and he and about five-hundred men were lost in a gas attack." Baxter said.

Hartwick was stunned. He had known a few men casually who had been killed in battle. But no one as close to him as Evans. He thought about Troy's big smile.

"Do you mean the establishment army is using nerve gas?" Hartwick asked. Trying to focus on the battle.

"Well, we don't know sir. General Picket says tear gas shouldn't work like that. It shouldn't kill a person. But we don't really know. Some of the men who made it back said that it looked like most of the men were shot.

We think whatever it was it caused confusion. They launched the gas, then the EA bastards went in when our guys were all disoriented and mowed them down.

I'm about thirty miles outside the city sir. I'm one of the relay Comms guys. Cell phones are down in the city so they get to me with two-ways. It takes a few minutes to get all the info. But right now, that's what we think happened."

"Are you sure they used gas?" Hartwick asked again. Not believing that it was possible.

"Yes sir. They definitely used something. Some of the men were just hit in the legs or shoulders. But they were all twisted up and dead. Word I'm getting sir is, like Picket said. Tear gas shouldn't have done that."

"Baxter, I'm going to call you back in a few minutes.

"Yes sir. I'll be out here until they tell me to come forward." Baxter answered.

When he hung up the phone he immediately called Admiral
Shock. Shock answered the phone expecting the call.

"Admiral this is General John Hartwick. Did you fucking
double cross me?" Hartwick said.

"What's going on General? And no, I did not." Shock
answered quickly.

"They just used gas on us in Richmond, just north of
Richmond on I-95." Hartwick said.

"General Hartwick, I will see what I can find out and call you
back in a few minutes."

In D.C. Shock called his group of fellow minded officers and
told them what had transpired. Then he called the president.

"Mr. President, we have made it clear to all sides that the
United States military would not allow the use of chemical, biologic
or radioactive weapons. We need to act."

President Hoxworth told Shock he was in favor, but wanted
to talk it over with Van Driessen first.

"Mr. President, I've spoken to Williams, Rodriguez and
several other generals and military leaders. We are not open to
much debate about this."

To President Hoxworth's surprise, Van Driessen wanted to
go further. He reasoned that they wouldn't be able to stop the war
anyway, and it was time to pick a side. When the President passed
the idea along to Shock he requested a personal meeting with the
President and Vice-President. He now knew that he could divulge
his plan.

President Hoxworth and Van-Driessen were both in agreement. If the NFA took Richmond, they would, along with the chairman of the Joint Chiefs, offer an unconditional surrender.

The President was already scheduled to hold an emergency press conference about the attack on Richmond. At Eight o'clock Eastern Time, the press was gathered.

The members of the press were briefed off camera before the official conference started. Admiral Shock spoke. He told them of the use of chemical weapons by the volunteer army. The army supported by all of the Democrats and a small number of long established Republicans.

They were told that the information was validated and that any suggestion that this was an attempt by the United States military, or the President of the United States to intervene on one side or the other would be considered treason and they would be arrested.

The President then spoke and told them that the military would retaliate, but only to stop the flow or further use of chemical weapons.

After the press conference ended Shock called Hartwick. He told them they were going to bomb long stretches of I-95 both south and north of Washington. He also told him the President and Vice-President were now aware of the plan to surrender, should Hartwick's army take Richmond.

If they were defeated, they would not intercede. But the bombing of 95 would give them a clear advantage and they should act accordingly.

Hartwick relayed the information to Picket. He was ordered to attack in full force in the morning.

On April 3rd the NFA tornado would be unleashed. With one-hundred and fifty-thousand trained troops at the front and another twenty-thousand who joined along the way, Picket attacked. Nearly one-hundred thousand more in reserve began to move forward.

Picket and his new young friend Jimmy Edward Burns, or Jeb moved near the front of the advance.

The battles raged from street to street and neighborhood to neighborhood inside Richmond. The NFA would often move a mile or two into an area where the fighting was already over. Locals had fought back and resisted the EA forces.

In other neighborhoods the battle would rage from house to house and street to street over several hours.

When it was quiet for an hour or two, Picket would send Jeb to the roof of some building to snipe at any enemy he could spot.

He would never let Jeb get in much danger. Though he did recognize that the young man was an excellent sniper, he was drawn to him because he reminded him of his own son.

At nineteen his son had been killed in one of the early battles near Atlanta Georgia. A striking similarity between the looks of the two had created a soft spot in his heart for young Jeb.

On April 6th Picket's forces took the Capital of Virginia and moved north eight miles to the exit where Troy Evans had been killed. The victory in Richmond was won. He called John Hartwick.

"General Hartwick, Richmond is ours. Our troops are in control of the city and surrounding suburbs all the way to 295. We are one-hundred miles from Washington D.C. What are your orders sir?"

"Thank you General Picket. I am heading to the airport. I will be landing in Richmond in about five hours.

Begin moving your forces to Arlington National Cemetery. We will meet tomorrow morning at seven at the tomb of the Unknown Soldier."

CHAPTER 14

VICTORY

A Large tent had been set up just outside of the Tomb.

The rain of the last few days had cleared and the morning was bright and cold.

The President of the United States, The Vice-President, the members of the military selected earlier, the Republican leader of the House, and the highest ranking Democrat from the House were in attendance. The Speaker had fled Washington for California as had many other Democrats.

When Hartwick walked in with Matt Davis, Jake Stahl, Jacob Picket, young Jeb, and a small group of other volunteer leaders from around the country, it was Admiral John Shock who stood first. He walked to Hartwick, saluted and shook his hand.

"Congratulations General. It is my pleasure and honor to finally meet you." The president and Vice-President then formed a line and shook Hartwick's hand and introduced themselves.

The media had been kept out of the area. They would be invited in for a press briefing at ten. The first order of business was to sign the surrender. It was a single piece of paper signed at the bottom by all in attendance. An unconditional surrender to the NFA or New Freedom Army.

President Hoxworth then spoke. We would like this transition to be as peaceful as possible. My first order of business will be to of course resign.

Hartwick stopped him. "Much will change in the coming days Mr. President. The military will not. We would also like to request that you and Vice-President Van-Driessen stay in office for the time being.

We are forming a committee of twelve men who will govern as the legislature. In eight months, on schedule, we intend to have elections. Voting will change. It will require an ID, and you must contribute to the nation in order to vote. The details of that will be worked out later."

"You mean, you want me to still be president?" Hoxworth asked, unable to hide the confusion on his face.

"Yes sir Mr. President." Hartwick answered. "We are not politicians. Hell, until just a year ago most of us weren't even soldiers. We want to get back to our lives. We want to get back to our families. We didn't ask for this. It was thrust upon us.

We will insist on changes. But we also want a peaceful transition. Half the nation voted for you. If you take out California, more than half."

Hoxworth looked to Van-Driessen. Always the pragmatist Van-Driessen answered without even being asked. "I'll do it. It's the smart move Mr. President."

"Thank you, General Hartwick. We have prepared an assessment of the current situation for you. This is Scott Alexander. He is a deputy director of analysts with the NSA."

Scott Alexander stood at the head of the long table.

"Good morning gentlemen. We started working with some of your military leaders last night. These estimates are early and subject to change. We also, of course, have analysts around the nation.

Over the last couple of days, we believe that your losses are over ten-thousand killed and thirty thousand wounded. Across the nation the number of your killed and wounded approaches one-hundred thousand men.

Most of these of course were not directly attached to your army. These are deaths from small skirmishes around the nation.

On the left, the battle of Richmond saw the loss of more than thirty-thousand killed and the number of wounded is unknown.

For the entirety of the civil war the death count is nearly the same as yours. Total killed in battle is roughly two-hundred thousand."

Hartwick interrupted. "That's actually much lower than I thought it would be."

"Sir, that is just killed in battle." Alexander said. "The total number of dead is unknown but well over two million and could be as high as five million dead."

"Oh shit. "How is that possible?" Hartwick asked.

"In the cities, suburbs and rural areas, insulin and antibiotics were hard to get. Many diabetics died. People with common infections, and no access to antibiotics died as well. There was also some death by starvation, but those almost certainly involved other aggravating circumstances.

This continues today, but it is better. Lifesaving surgeries were sometimes impossible as certain drugs became scarce.

The population of the nation before California seceded was three hundred and thirty million people.

With the loss of California and a sizable portion of Oregon, the population is now about two hundred and eighty-five million.

Over the last year, more than fifteen million more have either been forcibly evacuated or voluntarily left for California. About five million have left California for The United States. When we add the non-battle related deaths just mentioned, the population could be ten million fewer.

Prior to the war the Gross Domestic Product, that is, the entire economic output of the United States was approximately twenty-three trillion dollars. In California and the cities of Oregon aligned, the GDP was roughly three trillion dollars.

Our latest estimate is that the current U.S. GDP, without California, is something less than fifteen trillion dollars and could be as low as twelve trillion.

Our intelligence sources across the nation show that there are still active groups that will fight against you and the new nation.

We have identified over one hundred of these groups. Most are small. Just fifty people or so. A few are larger and becoming better organized in the last few months. I have much more information but I was told to keep it brief. That is the overall status of the nation at the moment."

When he had finished speaking Hartwick looked at Jake Stahl and Matt Davis. Both nodded. He stood up and began to speak as the titular head of the new nation.

"Thank you for that Mr. Alexander. You are fired. One of our first pieces of business will be to stop the United States Government from spying on its own people. I'm sure you are a fine man. But what you are doing is wrong and will no longer be necessary.

The FBI will help local law enforcement to find those who wish to continue this war. The CIA will continue to provide intelligence from foreign nations. But they will cease spying on American citizens."

Alexander started to stand up. "Should I leave now?" He asked nervously.

"No. It will take a few weeks for you to destroy all the intelligence you have gained on American citizens. You will transfer information on foreign nations or non-citizens to the FBI and CIA." Hartwick answered.

He then continued.

"Mr. Stahl will now speak. Jake was one of the first men I met when this battle for America started in Indiana, more than a year ago. Before that Jake was a…. Hell Jake, I just realized I don't know what you did before this. I'm sorry.

When I first met Jake he had this big beard. He was still big as a house, he just looked a little rough around the edges. But, he was a born leader and I guess it just kind of naturally happened that when we went into Indianapolis, someone had to be governor. He seemed like the logical choice. What did you do before this Jake?"

"I was an electrical engineer. I designed electronic components and computer programs for high definition camera systems for Hollywood California. I also have a degree in political science and history from Indiana University. My engineering degree is from Purdue." Stahl answered.

"Well shit." Matt Davis said. I thought you were one smart redneck. And I guess, I was right. I always thought I didn't get to be governor because I'm black!"

The men of the NFA laughed hysterically. Both sides could feel a great tension leave the room. Jake Stahl smiled and began to talk.

"When I became governor of Indiana we cut spending by more than seventy percent. That was mostly out of necessity at first. Then we realized things went along much as they had before. If it works there, it will work nationally. This is what we must do."

Stahl continued to talk. Van-Driessen, Matt Davis, and others talked as well. For the next few hours, the new nation began to take shape.

When it was time for the press conference Hartwick decided that it was best that only President Hoxworth speak. He notified the press that he would speak the next evening.

The president sent Air Force One to Indiana to get John Hartwick's wife and family. All agreed that John and his family should move into the White House. Hoxworth and his wife would live there as well.

Later that evening Hartwick made his first call as the leader of the new legislature.

He called Colby Ohlbinger.

CHAPTER 15

NEW NATIONS, NEW BEGINNINGS

J ohn Hartwick stood calmly at the podium in the press room of the White House.

For the first time in an interview, he was not nervous. The press was completely silent. No banter, even among themselves was evident. There was just one camera at the back of the room and another off to his left side.

"Good morning and thank you for coming. For those who don't know my name is John Hartwick.

Yesterday the surrender was signed by President Hoxworth, the majority and minority leaders of the Senate and The Chairman of the Joint Chiefs on behalf of the military.

Because we want this transition to go as smoothly as possible, President Hoxworth will continue as President and Vice-President Van Driessen will continue in his role.

All other politicians from all parties have been dismissed. I and a small group will act as the legislature for a short time. We hope to have elections soon. In those elections, only men or women who fought with us may run for office at the national level. This will be codified into law for the next twenty years.

Although there are many who sacrificed, we are the ones who risked our lives. We officially recognize the new nation of California. The boundaries are still in dispute, but we hope to resolve that peacefully. Over the coming days and weeks, we will work to build the nation that we fought for.

For those of you watching at home, after this press conference, all television and radio will continue with President Colby Ohlbinger of the new nation of California.

I have spoken briefly with him this morning, and we both want the fighting to end. He has promised me there will be no attempts to expand their borders and to resolve the existing disputes peacefully.

I will caution you that there is no guarantee that will happen. But we have his word that he will try and he has my word and that of President Hoxworth.

After President Ohlbinger speaks, Reverend John Robert Ross of Texas will address the nation.

And now I will take questions."

Hartwick called on a first reporter in the front row.

"Mr. President, er, sorry, what is your title to be?"

"My name is John Hartwick. You may call me Mr. Hartwick."

"Mr. Hartwick, what is your mission? What were you fighting for and what changes can we expect. Not just as reporters, but also as citizens?"

"When I first became involved in this fight my mission was to get back to work so I could make my house payment. At the time I felt the nation was on a bad path. But I was never politically active. As time went by I started to think about what I was fighting for.

I wish to live free. That is the first thing. I want to live in a nation where I am free to speak my mind. Where I cannot lose my job because of politically correct speech.

If I disagree with someone, I do not wish to be called a racist, bigot or idiot. With those accusations of racism or bigotry in the past, you could lose your job. That is not free.

I also don't want to live in fear of my government. If I make a mistake on my taxes, I should not fear losing my home.

If I accidently spill oil in my yard I should not fear a team of armed men from the EPA.

You may think I'm exaggerating, but things like this were beginning to happen.

If I am to pay taxes, my work and contribution should be acknowledged. There are hundreds and hundreds of massive government agencies. Many of them have little accountability for the money that they spend and a horrendous record of success.

The states were often duplicating these efforts. The EPA and the Department of Education are not just national organizations. Each state duplicates the effort. That must end.

I also do not wish to be the victim of another person's misfortune. That kind of thinking just creates more victims and fewer people like myself to bail them out.

If your parents brought you to this country illegally twenty years ago, why does their crime, and their children's victimhood extend to me? Why must I pay for their mistake?

But it's more than just the taxes and laws. There is something else that I think is wrong, and I should add, every single member of our committee believes this as well.

When I sit down to watch a movie or a television show with my children, I don't want to cringe or be angry. I don't want

Hollywood telling me I'm ignorant because I disagree with the social justice cause of the moment.

I'm sick and tired of going to movies that are all the same. The white man is bad, the businessman is evil, and the Republican is evil. In these same movies the single woman, the gay man or the black man is always the hero. Why?

Why does the Hollywood culture come at me and my family instead of helping me? How is this good for the nation?

The schools are the same way. Teaching math, English and history are all just afterthoughts. And even these subjects are sprinkled with politics.

My eight-year-old daughter doesn't need to be taught that she is responsible for global warming. Or that her father's corporation is evil and killing people.

It's not true, and it's too much to put on a kid. If you can't teach them the necessary tools, what the hell are they ever going to be able to do about it anyway?

I think gay people should be able to live together in peace. I don't believe that every other gendered couple has the right to adopt children. I don't think it is right to experiment on people for social justice causes.

For that, I am, well not anymore, but before we won, I would have been ostracized.

By who? By a phony cultural push that gave people license to disrespect me or otherwise abuse me because we disagree.

And when I watch the news, I want the truth. A free press is important. But you have to tell the truth.

For years you have reported on rumors. You have accused politicians of crimes with no evidence. And let's be honest, you reported these things against conservatives much more than you did liberals.

I also don't want the news and flow of information in this nation controlled by a handful of massive corporations.

I guess to summarize, we fought for a government that stays small and out of our lives. We fought for a government that realizes we are the reason for its very existence.

We do not wish to have our money take for causes we do not agree with. We don't wish to become second-hand victims by the simple virtue of our success.

We wish to live as one nation. This nation. We want the best for the world. But we cannot hand out free stuff to every person who manages to fight their way in here.

We were rapidly approaching the point where our ability to help was being seriously threatened. We weren't going to be able to help even ourselves.

Those are the reasons we fought. And those are the things we will fix."

He stopped and waited for a hand to raise. Then several hands slowly started to rise.

"Mr. Hartwick, what restrictions are you putting on us? The press?"

"Only one. You must report the truth. If you are to call yourselves news, you must report the news. You cannot have opinions on news programs.

On your opinion programs, you are in the public. You cannot accuse people of crimes that they have not been charged with in courts.

You also cannot undermine our government. I realize that is a hazy statement, but be careful. You cannot suggest that we are illegitimate.

We fought, and our friends, family and associates died for this cause."

The questions continued for an hour. Hartwick would not allow another single question at the end of the allotted time. He closed and walked away.

Fifteen minutes later, in Sacramento Colby Ohlbinger was standing at the podium. The press was all from California. He had made sure what each question was to be. It was all to be scripted.

After watching Hartwick for the first few minutes he began scribbling a speech of his own. He needed to respond.

Every sentence he added, he checked with Scotch Anderson. His respect for the man had grown immensely. When Anderson agreed with him too readily, Colby would push back.

Over the last two years, he had matured. He had begun to realize the awesome responsibility he had been handed. He knew that he had taken it more than had earned it. But that would change.

Many nights he would wake up screaming about what he had done to Steve Oxley. He knew it would always be with him now. In some ways it was comforting. He knew at last that he was not a psychopath.

He checked his notes one last time. He was now late. Only by a minute. But it was one more thing he was trying to change. He needed discipline. Only Anderson would provide any challenge to him at all. He would have to discipline himself.

He walked to the podium to thunderous applause from the press. His face showed no reaction at all. He just stared at them. The press, now thoroughly confused sat quickly.

"I want to first thank General Hartwick for his press conference. I would also like to thank President Hoxworth for allowing us to broadcast this press conference to our family and friends in The United States.

After listening to that speech at the beginning of his press conference I am happy to hear that they want many of the same things we want. Maybe that has always been true.

But we differ greatly in how we want to accomplish these things.

We believe if an illness befalls a family, it should not bankrupt them. We also believe that if a person works, if a person does a job, that person should be paid enough to enjoy a basic standard of living.

We don't believe that if you flip hamburgers you should be able to avoid a big house and support a family. But you should at least be able to support yourself, shouldn't you?

Too often in the past we would hear from our friends on the right that these jobs were starter jobs. Jobs for teenagers never meant to support a person. Well, what if that's the only job you can get?

We also believe that education is the path to success. Not just for you as individuals, but for our nation. We will strive to introduce free college for everyone in the next couple of years. That will take some adjustment on everyone's part, but we know we can do this.

We also believe that this planet is precious, and that we have to protect it. And we will do that. We wish to trade with our American cousins. We know that they wish to trade with us as well. But this is going to be a different country than what many of you are used too.

Here you will find not just freedom, but security. Secure in the fact that your children will not be burdened by debt from their education. Secure in the fact that your children and grandchildren will grow up in a healthy environment. That global warming will not cause them the incredible economic hardship that is predicted. I will reach out to our friends in Europe, Asia and all over the world to join us in a working treaty to save the planet.

Last, and perhaps most important, I beg of General Hartwick and President Hoxworth, let the people go. We welcome our friends from the United States who would like to join us. Come! Bring your talents and your energy for a wonderful society with you. We need you and we want you. We welcome you with open arms.

When the speech was ended Colby took just a few questions. It was clear to Hartwick and Hoxworth that they were scripted. They watched until it ended and then John Robert Ross, a preacher from Texas began to speak.

Hartwick was nervous, but he remembered his good friend, Troy Evans. Evans had liked JR Ross before they had even met. Once he had met him he not only liked him more, he trusted him more. Hartwick had also been largely persuaded. But they had given this man great power. His only hope was that the preacher from Texas would help to unite the nation.

Ross had decided to give his speech from the pulpit of his church in Dallas. The church could easily seat twenty-thousand people. It was full every Sunday. But tonight there were thousands more. They were standing in the aisles and around the floor in front of the pulpit.

"Good Evening my fellow Americans. Good evening all of my brothers and sisters who may be watching from the new nation of California. The war is over."

Thunderous applause rose from the congregation. Ross tried to speak but the applause took several minutes to die down.

"The war is over, but the battle between good and evil will continue as it always has and always will until the good Lord decides it is time to end.

We have a great opportunity ahead of us. Though many millions are struggling, the future is bright. If, however, we begin to blame each other, then that bright future will quickly fade.

This new nation, this new version of The United States cannot be divided. It will not stand if we are divided. There can be no more black men, white men, and Hispanic or Asian women. This must be a nation of individuals. A nation of free men and women.

I am an evangelical Christian Pastor. I would like for all men and women in this nation to be Christians. But it cannot come through the government. It cannot be forced. Every man must come to God and peace on his own.

Every man must be free to pursue the desires of his heart and mind. There can be no dignity without freedom. There can be no salvation and no peace of soul without the freedom to gain these things on your own free will and by your own efforts.

The new nation of California is becoming prosperous. Our new nation will also be prosperous. I hope and pray that both nations are blessed by God.

But even though California is now prospering, it is not yet back to where it was before this war started. The petty differences that existed between us were allowed to fester. They were allowed to become so divisive that there seemed no path to peace between us.

Those petty differences led us to attempt to destroy the greatest nation the world has ever known.

If we allow these divisions and past hurts to consume us, we will not prosper either.

I know that some of these differences were driven by passionate beliefs. But that passion was too often exploited. Exploited by business owners, politicians, and others with an agenda.

And so we have fought. Hundreds of thousands lost their lives. Millions more have lost their homes, jobs and the peace of the normal way of life.

Let us all be humble in our victory and compassionate to our former enemies. For if we do not do this, what have we really gained?"

Three months later

"What do you think John?" Victor Van-Driessen was on a first-name and friendly basis with John Hartwick. The two had worked tirelessly over the last few months.

"About how we are doing?" Hartwick asked.

"No, about the war. Your life has been turned upside down. Now here you sit. There are a lot of people that want you to run for president in a few years. I asked because I'm not that much different.

I got into politics just a few years ago. Never thought I'd be Vice-President of the United States. I also never imagined until a couple of years ago that there would be a civil war. Was it worth it?"

"I think so. But then I look at California and how well they are doing. They have almost everything they wanted. It looks like we're finally on the right track.

But I can't help wondering if the left were right all along. Hell, the population over the, with what we keep sending and the people still going on their own, I hear it's pushing seventy million people. So it makes me wonder if we did the right thing."

"It won't last. That's one of the things I wanted to put on the agenda today. The president and I have been talking about it quite a bit. Matt Davis is working on the issue as well." Van-Driessen said.

"What is it?"

"The reason they are doing so well is they have no debt. They just walked away from it. All the initial money they made to support their own currency was U.S. dollars. From the port tariffs. Now they are trading with much of Asia. China is helping them out quite a bit.

On the other hand. We are saddled with nearly thirty-trillion in debt. The fine people of The Free State of California are responsible for a good portion of that."

"So what are you suggesting we do?" Hartwick asked.

"We have another big problem as well."

"I think we have a bunch of them Vic." Hartwick said.

"Not like this one. I got a call from the president this morning. He got an interesting call last night. Two calls actually. One from the prime minister of France, the other from Germany.

I wanted to wait until we met with the committee tonight, but it can't wait."

"What is it?"

"France and Germany have formed an alliance. They ask the president if we were still in NATO.

Tomorrow morning they are going to declare war on Austria, Poland, Hungary and most of the rest of Eastern Europe. France and Germany are also forming an alliance with Iran, Iraq, Kuwait and a few other Middle Eastern countries. They are looking for support from the Saudis and Egypt as well. It looks like we have another world war on our hands."

Hartwick dropped his head and sighed.

After a few minutes, he looked up to the vice-president and said.

"The world keeps turning."

Hartwick nodded.

"And the world keeps burning." He looked at Van-Driessen and finally realized the dilemma.

"So if we try to go after California to get them to pay the debt, it could lead to another war."

Van-Driessen nodded. "Yes. And then if it falls apart in Europe we may not be in a position to help there."

"So what do you and the president suggest?" Hartwick said.

"It's going to be up to the committee. If we can hold out a few more months, we can leave it up to the new Congress.

But our suggestion, and the military leadership is largely in agreement on this one, is that we might want to sit out this world war and focus on rebuilding the nation."

"I suppose that makes the most sense. I'm no historian Vic, but I have learned one thing. Things change."

Victor Van-Driessen nodded again. "Yes, they do John. Things change."

Made in the USA
Las Vegas, NV
09 April 2022

47172670R00173